A DUKE
OF A TIME

TAMARA

Gill

COPYRIGHT

A Duke of a Time
The Wayward Woodvilles, Book 1
Copyright © 2022 by Tamara Gill
Cover Art by Wicked Smart Designs
Editor Grace Bradley Editing, LLC

ISBN: 978-0-6454177-1-5

CHAPTER
ONE

1805, Berkeley Square, London

Greyson Everett, Marquess of Cadmael, clenched his fists and ground his teeth as his father continued his tirade against him. He schooled his features, knowing too well that to insult and anger his father more by arguing or disagreeing with his views never ended well for him. He had learned a long time ago to keep his mouth shut or face physical repercussions.

Even so, the demand his father put upon him was beyond anything he had ever dished out before. Perhaps the rumors were true that were circulating about London. That his father was turning senile. That the nasty old duke was losing his mind. His decree certainly made Greyson think that was the case.

"Northamptonshire? That is where you're sending me?" He took a calming breath, the urge to stand, to go nose to nose with the waspish duke who had few friends—and fewer relatives who wanted to ever be around him—grew.

As the spiteful words continued to rain down on

Greyson, he promised himself he would never be a father such as his. A mean and nasty, violent and vindictive bastard whom he loathed.

He could only thank his dearest mother was no longer around to suffer such a union.

"You," his father spat, pointing his chubby, stubby finger in his direction, "will go to Northamptonshire. You will work at Mr. Woodville's manor house, and you will work hard and sweat out the privilege you have since you're not respectful of it."

"I gained a mistress, Father. I enjoy entertainments offered to us during The Season and my club. Many gentlemen in town do the same. There is nothing wrong with that."

"Well, your mistress is no more, for I'll not pay for any whore or any more gambling or rutting or whatever it is that you do about town all day."

Greyson shuffled in his chair, fisting his hands in his lap. What he really wanted to do was punch his bastard father in the nose and walk out. Rutting and gambling indeed. His father made it sound as if that was all he did, and while he did quite a lot of it, it was never with women who were not willing to lift their skirts, and never with an unmarried maid.

It was not like he was rutting up against the side of a building in St. James without a by your leave. His father ought to be proud that his trysts were private, not fodder for gossips.

"Do you mean you are cutting off my allowance?" he asked, making a mental calculation on how much money he did have left in hand. Not quite a hundred pounds, which if his father followed through on his threat, would keep him fed and clothed at least in Northamptonshire, but little else. He would normally blow through five times that amount on a night when the need arose.

Which wasn't as often as his father was making out.

"Indeed I am, and you will be leaving for the Woodville Estate in Northamptonshire following our discussion via stagecoach. I have instructed your valet to pack items of clothing that will be suitable as a farmhand and some funds to see you through your journey up north. Do not try to run, do not try to seek help from any friends you know. I have men watching you who will put a stop to such things. You will learn your lesson, boy, and you will learn it the hard way."

Greyson narrowed his eyes at his sire. How was it that he was from his loins? How was it that anyone would have ever married such a heinous, nasty piece of cow dung?

"I think this is an overreaction to your son who gained a mistress. I could have instead caused scandal by having an illicit affair with some matron, or an unhappily married woman in our society. No sane father reacts like you do. I enjoy my freedom as a young and unmarried lord. Just as I'm certain you did as well. What is wrong with you?"

His father's eyes widened before his face turned a deep shade of red. His Grace fisted his hands at his sides, and Greyson could see them shaking. "Do not ever speak back to me again. You have responsibility and respectability to keep for the Derby dukedom. I will not have my only son making a fool and mockery out of our name. Never in the history of the family has anyone released their seed outside the bonds of marriage, and I will not have you do the same."

Greyson took a calming breath. "I'm careful, Father, and with the precautions I take, I'm certain that will not happen."

"Lady Francesca the Earl of Lincoln's daughter, is an heiress and attractive enough to tempt you, I'm sure. Upon your return, you will court her and marry the chit. She will make a perfect duchess."

"I will not," he returned hotly, having heard enough. "You cannot make me marry anyone whom I do not wish to." He paused. "Not to mention her face resembles the horses she loves so very dearly."

"You will court and marry her upon your arrival home once you have learned your lesson, and I am satisfied you're a man of character and not loose morals. You will marry a woman who is a good Christian with high principles, connections, and wealth. I shall hear of nothing else about it. Do you understand, boy?"

Greyson swallowed the bile that rose in his throat and stood. "I understand perfectly. I also want to state that you're a bastard, and if I never lay eyes on you again, I will not be disappointed."

His father smirked, and it more resembled a snarl. "I'm glad you finally understand your father. Safe travels, son," he said, dismissing him with a flick of his hand before he sat himself down at his desk and continued on with his bookwork.

Greyson turned on his heel and stormed from the room, not bothering to close the door behind him. This was utterly uncalled for and not to mention absurd. Northamptonshire indeed. And to work as a farmhand, who had ever thought of such an insult to a duke's son.

He went directly to his room and found his valet packing up the last of his things. He looked at the small trunk with distaste. "What have you packed me, Thompson?" he asked his loyal servant, who had come to work for the ducal estate as a young, orphaned boy and was his friend long before he became his valet.

"I found some old gardener's clothing in the attic upstairs. There were some boots and a worn greatcoat, which should do you well up in Northamptonshire. It will be colder up north than down here in London."

Greyson spied the second small bag near the armoire. "What is in that bag?" he asked, pulling at his cravat and changing into a set of clothing laid out on his bed. There was little point in staying in London, not if his father had men watching his every move and was determined he would do as he was told.

And he would, he would prove to his father that he would not only go to the Woodville Estate, but he would work hard just so his father could not say he did not. He would never let the bastard win this war. Nor would he be returning and marrying Lady Francesca. He shuddered at the thought.

"That is for me, my lord. I am coming with you." Thompson gestured to his clothing, which Greyson had not noticed until now was similar to what he was changing into. "I will work alongside you and keep an eye on you. You are a marquess, after all, and the future Duke of Derby. I'm sure I'm not the only one in London who wishes for your safe and speedy return."

Greyson sighed, annoyance thrumming through him that he had not been able to dismiss his mistress himself. That his father had carried out the duty left him uneasy. Was she safe? Did he give her any funds to keep her secure until she found another protector? "Send word to Cissie and ensure she's safe and well. Send funds too and apologize to her on my behalf."

"Of course, my lord." Thompson went about writing a

letter, and Greyson finished changing his clothing. The trews were made of coarse fabric, less comfortable than his silk breeches. Not to mention the shirt was stained and had an odd scent about it.

He wrinkled his nose, hating to think what rodent had climbed over the clothing he now wore.

Thompson blotted the missive and sealed it. "I shall have this sent out today, my lord. I will return for the bags posthaste."

Greyson nodded, watching as Thompson left the room. He strode to his desk, found his purse holding the last of his allowance, and pocketed it. His hat sat on a nearby sideboard, and he swooped it up, laying it atop his head. Looking about the room, he shook his head at the thought of the journey he was about to embark upon. How foolish his father was being. How utterly narrowminded and behind the times.

It was 1805, for heaven's sake. Was it not time for his father to live in the new century upon them and stop living in the Georgian England he was so very fond of?

Thompson returned, picking up the trunk. "Shall we go, my lord? The hackney is out front to take us to the Swan with Two Necks Inn to catch the stagecoach."

"Yes," he said, taking one last look about his room. He could do this, and he would. And in the process, he would make his father look the fool for making him do such a thing.

The Duke of Derby glanced up from his desk and watched as his son strode past the library door and out of the town house, his valet close on his heels.

His steward stepped into the room, having been privy to

the duke's plans and waiting for his son to depart. "So he is off then, Your Grace. Do you think your plan will work?"

His Grace fought not to laugh. "Oh, yes, I do. If my son has a soft spot for anything, it is an attractive woman, and I know for a fact that Anne Woodville has sired five handsome daughters. One of them will tempt Greyson, and finally, my revenge on that woman will be complete."

His steward nodded, but like most in the duke's life, he did not know that Anne Woodville, daughter to an earl, had thrown him over for a country gentleman, no better than a farmer.

"What if your son falls for one of the Woodville daughters and elopes? Will not that make Anne a winner yet again, since her daughter will one day be a duchess?"

That was the beauty of his plan. Anne Woodville despised him now, he had ruined her father, and they had lost all their money not long after Anne had married Woodville. The last person she would allow her daughter to marry would be his son, when she found out who he was, of course.

"Anne will not allow a union between the pair, first because she will believe him a farmhand, too lowly for her daughter. But second, she will know it was me behind his arrival and when she realizes who he is, her hatred of me will stop any marriage between the pair. Even if they do elope, the merging of our families will hurt Anne, and that is enough for me, not that I think that will occur."

"And your son's heart, Your Grace? The young lady may be injured by this plan too."

"True," he agreed, shrugging. "But no one turns from the Duke of Derby, makes me look the fool by marrying a man not fit to wipe my boots. I have waited many years to hit at Anne Woodville, and that time has finally arrived. It is unfortunate that my son is such a failing, and therefore has to be used in such a scheme, but I always win, and it is time everyone knew this, no matter how many years pass where they think they are safe from my ire." *No one bests the Duke of Derby. No one.*

CHAPTER
TWO

Miss Hailey Woodville stood at the library window and watched as two new farmhands jumped down from the cart they had sent into Grafton to pick up. Her steward mentioned they had traveled for work all the way from London, and she was interested in seeing how these city workers would get on at their farm.

The crops were coming along nicely this time of year, and would soon be ready for harvest, a busy time for everyone, not just in their county. Her father came to stand at her side, peering out the window.

"Ah, are these the two new workers you mentioned?" he asked her, slipping on his spectacles to see them more clearly.

"Yes, although the tall one doesn't look like he'd be much use in the fields. Look at his hands, Papa," she stated.

Her father frowned. "I do not see anything out of the ordinary about his hands. What do you see, my dear?"

Hailey could see they looked as soft as butter even from this distance. Had these men ever worked on a farm or in a stable, or had they only done bookwork in an office until today? From the looks of their confused, unimpressed faces, they seemed as interested in the farm as a lion would in a cage.

"I do not think these London folks will do well here at all. The shorter one may suit. He at least looks a little less lost than the tall one, but then, not by much."

"Are we going to lay a bet?" her father asked, mischief twinkling in his tired, gray eyes.

"A pound says that the tall one breaks first and leaves within a month," she said, always willing to wager.

Her father held out his hand, and she shook it. "Deal." She smiled as he went and sat on the settee before the fire. "How are the estate books, my dear? Everything in hand?" he asked, sighing as he lifted his legs along the settee to rest.

"All is doing very well, Papa. The crops are coming along, and we're finishing up the repairs on several cottages in Grafton this month and those of the tenant farms before the weather turns cool. We will be well placed for winter and then my first season in town next year."

"Oh yes, of course. I had forgotten you're to leave us all for the much-fashionable London. Your mama is certainly looking forward to a Season in town. Have you been practicing your curtsy you're to give to the queen?"

Hailey smiled, sitting across from her papa. "I have, and I think I will do well enough and not embarrass anyone."

Her papa reached out and clasped her hand, squeezing it a little. "You would never embarrass any of your family. You're a good girl."

Hailey smiled, but her stomach twisted at the compliment that she did not entirely deserve, not in her opinion anyway. She was a good daughter and worked hard with the steward to ensure everything ran smoothly at Woodville House. Her father would prefer to bird-watch than do the books, and her mother longed for society and was forever seeking out gossip in Grafton.

But lately, life here in Grafton and Northamptonshire was no longer all that she longed for. Looking after the estate, ensuring the farm ran smoothly and that all her sisters had whatever they needed was a lot of work. Not to mention having to socialize in Grafton, visit friends, but it was always the same. Nothing exciting ever happened or changed.

At one and twenty, she wanted to find a husband, marry, and have children. She wanted to travel and love with her whole heart, have a passionate love affair like the ones she read about in her romantic novels. The London Season could not come soon enough, and for all those things to come to fruition.

"I suppose Mr. Oak will be in soon to introduce us to the new workers. Are you going to stay?" she asked her father, knowing he rarely did his duty and met the servants.

"Not today, my dear. I'm off to the river. I'm hoping to spy a Blue-winged Teal, which has been elusive to me this year, but I'm determined," he said, lifting himself out of the chair, bussing her cheek before striding to the door.

"I'll see you at dinner then," she called after him, his footsteps echoing down the hallway toward the back of the house.

"Right you are," he called back.

Hailey sighed, staring at the fire and debating putting wood on it herself since it had been an age since a servant had been in to service it. She stood, leaning down to the fire and placing two logs onto the flames, kneeling before it a moment as she watched the yellow flame lick the wood.

"I beg your pardon, Miss Woodville. The new stable hand and laborer are here to meet you."

Hailey started at the sound of Mr. Oak, having not heard them enter the house. She stood, her foot catching on the hem of her dress before she stumbled and righted herself.

Hailey came to an undignified halt just as her eyes alighted on the tall farmhand she'd seen outside. The very one she had bet with her father would last less than the shorter, stubbier type of fellow who looked used to hard work. She looked up...and up. Hailey schooled her features as her mind reeled at the man's broad, muscular physique, his presence that commanded respect.

When did servants start to look as this one did?

"Miss Woodville, this is Mr. Thompson and Mr. Everett. We were going to use both in the stable and in the fields as required. As you know, Miss Julia has recently saved another horse from the markets in town, and we could use the help in the stalls. If you're in agreement, of course."

Hailey smoothed down her dress and came up to them, smiling in welcome. "Good afternoon, Mr. Thompson. Mr. Everett. I hope the journey to Northamptonshire wasn't too taxing for you, and you're ready to work."

"We are ready, Miss Woodville," Mr. Thompson agreed, elbowing his friend, who remained mute.

"Of course, we will work well enough, I'm sure," the tall one said, tedium in his tone. He glanced about the room, and she could see that he looked less than impressed by the worn but homely furnishings. Hailey looked about herself, seeing nothing wrong with the room.

She narrowed her eyes. "Good, I hope you're both ready to work, for we do not tolerate lazy Londoners in this part of England. I hope I've made myself clear," she said, hating that she had allowed her annoyance at the tall one to make her words harsher than they ought to have been.

"We will work hard, we assure you, Miss Woodville," Thompson said.

Mr. Everett stared at her, a small twist to his lips. Which, much to Hailey's annoyance, she noticed had a very nice shape about them. Were they soft to touch? She fisted her hands at her sides and scowled. "Dinner is served in a room just off the kitchen for the staff at Woodville House. You will bed down at night in the stables. There is a room with cots allocated for outside staff. You will not be cold, as we have a fire burning whenever the nights are chill here, and there are plenty of blankets to go around. If you have any trouble, please let Mr. Oak or myself know of it, and we will look into your inquiry. There is no fighting here. You will be dismissed instantly if that occurs." She smiled, but even Hailey knew the gesture was less than friendly. "I wish you both well, and welcome to Woodville's."

The tall one scoffed, all but rolling his eyes. "Thank you for your kind welcome, Miss Woodville," he said, his voice unlike the man at his side. There was a deepness about it, cultured even, that did not go with a man who worked hard for his money. Not to mention bored.

Hailey watched them depart. She would have to keep an eye on the new men, especially the tall, handsome one who seemed to think himself well above anyone else, even her.

Not that she liked to loft it over anyone, but she was the eldest daughter of a gentleman, which gave her a little authority in life.

She walked to the window, the sound of Mr. Oak talking to the men about their duties as they headed over to the stables muffled. Mr. Thompson seemed interested and replying to what her steward was saying. The other one,

Mr. Everett, looked as if he could not care an ounce what he was being told.

Hailey shook her head. Yes, she'd be a pound wealthier by the end of the month, and she had little doubt that it would happen within four weeks if not seven days.

THREE

G reyson shoveled yet another scoop of horse shit into the small cart, sweat poured down his skin, and a terrible, stale, unwashed stench wafted from him that he had only ever smelled when passing people in the East End of London. Which, he wanted to point out, was not very often.

Thompson shoveled away, seemingly content to do the hard labor, even though he was a valet and no longer needed to do such menial chores.

"I do not know how we can continue to allow such degradation just to please my father. I think I would rather be disowned than have to endure another day of this." He leaned on his shovel, wiping his brow.

Thompson rested his shovel against the horse stall wall and walked over to where a flask of water was sitting for their use. "Prove your father wrong, Everett," his valet said, using his family name instead of Lord Cadmael, who he was until he took over the dukedom. Right at this moment, he couldn't help but hope that was sooner rather than later.

Greyson wanted to snarl at the unfairness of it all. That

he was to endure such hardship was unreasonable, and he ought to put a stop to it. Confront his father and demand the bastard accept that heirs of age took mistresses and enjoyed London and all it had to offer. That the duke was a prude should not be his fault or something he had to suffer for.

"How are ye going in here?" the foreman of the stable workers asked, coming into the stall and inspecting their progress. "Ye are not doing too bad since you're from London. Not many from those parts come here," he mentioned, looking at them both.

Greyson assumed the man expected an answer, but he could not form a reply. Not unless he wanted to be sacked a day after his arrival.

Thompson broke the awkward silence. "We are appreciative for the employment, Mister..."

The foreman waved down his question. "Morris is well enough. We have no airs or graces here. Not below stairs in any case."

"Well, we thank you, Mr. Morris," Thompson said, frowning at Greyson.

He managed a nod, but little else.

"Once ye are done in here, four other stalls are needing a muck out and fresh hay laid for the horses. Then ye can move outside and load up what's left of the hay from last year's harvest. We're looking to store it in the old barn near the river. It'll leave the new barn built last summer empty for the new harvest."

How thrilling, Greyson thought, having never cared for what happened on gentry or noble estates, so long as the yields were good, that the tenant farmers were happy, and he had enough money to keep himself living in the life that he was accustomed.

One day of this life was enough for him to endure. He was probably fortunate he had been born wealthy, and this short foray in the wilds of Northamptonshire was not permanent.

Like Thompson stated, he should not allow his father to win this war. He would work here at the estate and throw the bastard's order back in his face. Prove to him that he could do anything, even muck out stables and move hay from hayloft to hayloft if necessary.

"Keep on with it then," Morris said, moving down the stables and checking the many horses stalled within them. Some of the mounts were better than Greyson thought they would be, considering one of the daughters of the house had saved them from the local market.

"You must try at least to pretend to be one of the workers here, Everett. I have no doubt, someone among us knows who we are, and they will inform the duke if it's thought you are not pulling your weight."

Greyson picked up his shovel again. "I'm doing what is asked of me. I never stated that I would look thrilled about it or become a conversationalist."

Thompson's lips thinned, and Greyson knew what his valet was trying to say. Be less judging of his circumstances before his father found out.

"What did you think of Miss Woodville?" Thompson asked him. Greyson knew that such a conversation with one's valet was not appropriate to many gentlemen, but he had known Thompson since they were children, and he had always classed him more as a friend than a servant. He knew without a speck of doubt that he could trust him absolutely.

"She was a bit of an ape leader, did you not think? A

little too rammish for my liking, but fetching enough, I suppose."

"Come, man," Thompson scoffed, leaning on his shovel once again. "I almost swallowed my tongue when I saw her."

Greyson supposed it was Miss Woodville's eyes that he noticed first, bright and wide, and all-seeing. Something about the woman ought to put him on guard. She was intelligent, certainly, and she spoke with authority and in a forthright manner, which showed she was educated. But a bluestocking through and through and one whom he had no desire to taunt.

"I daresay if she were to have a London Season, there would be many who would flock to her skirts," Thompson added, nodding eagerly.

"I'm sure some gentleman or mayhap even a baron may offer for her hand. However, from the looks of the modest estate, I do not think there is a lot of money for a dowry. How many daughters did the gentleman have? And no sons, is that correct?"

"That is correct," Thompson answered. "There are five daughters in total. I suppose that all will need to marry well, but I have little doubt they will garner offers from respectable men. They are not poor, Everett," he said.

Greyson held up his hands in surrender. "I'm merely stating we do not know their financial circumstances," he said, the stench of horse shit going some way to mask his own disgusting stink.

"I can see by your face that you're disapproving and judging them."

Greyson schooled his features to one of indifference. "I wish them all well, all five of the sisters, just as I wish myself out of this hovel and down to the river so I may wash. I smell, Thompson. Can you smell me from over there?"

Thompson threw back his head and laughed. Greyson looked at him, nonplussed. "Oh, yes you do, my lord," he whispered. "And I cannot wait for you to bathe either. At this moment, I doubt my nostrils will ever recover from the odor seeping from your direction."

Greyson shoveled another scoop into the barrow. "Get to work, Thompson," he growled, ignoring his valet's chuckle and concentrating instead on finishing his work for the day so he could clean up. His father would pay for this punishment. He would complete the order, return to London and rut his life away until his father passed. Then and only then would he marry a woman if he married at all. And he certainly would not be marrying Lady Francesca as his father wished. He promised. He would get the last laugh, not the duke.

CHAPTER

FOUR

T he afternoon soon gave way to dusk, and as per
her usual routine, Hailey wandered down to the
river to sketch the birds and the few ducks who
made it their home as they settled for the evening.

She would miss this when she entered society next year,
make her curtsy to the queen, and become a debutante on
the prowl for a husband. She hoped to find a gentleman
who was smart and no-nonsense like herself. Handsome
would also be nice, but she wasn't holding out too much
hope on that score.

Her footsteps skidded to a halt, and she stifled a gasp
when the sight of Mr. Everett came into view. She slipped
behind an old oak tree's trunk, its branches stretched out
over the river, throwing dappling sunlight upon his person.
Her surprise was soon replaced by annoyance. This was not
where the servants were allowed to bathe. What on earth
was the man doing?

She felt her eyes widen as he turned, his torso visible for
her to marvel at. Water licked its way down his chest,
rippling over his muscular stomach. His arms flexed and

pulled tight as he ran his fingers through his hair, pushing it away from a face chiseled to perfection like some Greek god. She shook her head, hating herself for ogling, but she could not take her eyes from his arms. She would long remember their size. Certainly, when she was alone in her room later this evening, she may even sketch what she could remember.

Hailey swallowed a sigh as his hands washed his front, scrubbing away the day's grime. He had a feathering of hair on his chest, something she had not seen before on a man.

She bit her lip. She shouldn't be looking. She certainly should not be watching a stable hand during a private moment, but nor could she seem to move. Her fingers clutched the tree, flexing about the bark as if it were his muscles beneath her hands—hard and rough.

"I know you're there," he called, his voice low and bored as if women watching him in a river were an everyday occurrence that he often had to call them out on.

She stepped into view and walked to the edge of the water, sitting on an old fallen tree where she normally sat. Alone. He would not best her, nor would he intimidate her on her own property. This was her river and her drawing location. He may leave if he wished.

"I thought to give you privacy, but since you know that I'm here, I'll take my seat."

He lifted his gaze, and she thought for a moment a twinkling of amusement entered his dark-blue eyes before he blinked, and it was gone.

"Should a gently bred young lady be watching a man bathe? I think not," he stated.

Heat kissed her cheeks, and she marked his point. Still, his insolence toward her, the boredom in his tone at her being nearby, irked her pride, and she could not allow him to think he had gained the advantage of who was in fact in charge here.

"Probably not, but then this is my river, and I sketch birds every evening in this spot. A fact you would know had you asked Morris if you were allowed to bathe in this location." She pointed to a bend in the river where high reeds gave privacy on the bank. "Most of the workers bathe and swim in that part of the river, not here. Never here," she said, crossing her arms over her chest and raising her chin. There, she had told him and explained how he was in the wrong and not her.

He shook his head, walking toward the bank. More of his body became visible—his torso right down to where his skintight breeches hugged his waist. Taut muscles in the shape of a V slipped beneath his breeches, and Hailey lost the ability to think.

The world before her blurred, and all she could focus on was where his breeches outlined the very nature of the man, including his appendages.

He came up before her, not saying a word. Hailey lifted her gaze, taking in every nuance of his person. Her hands itched to touch to see if his muscles were indeed as hard and well-formed as her eyes were telling her they were.

Good heavens, he was like a god, not a man. Tall and commanding. He oozed authority, and yet, he was a stable worker. A farmhand. Her servant in all respects.

"I did look in on that part of the river and found this area more to my liking." He snatched the notebook from her hand. Hailey gaped at his audacity and tried to take it from his fingers. He held it above her head, ignoring her pummeling fists as he opened the book and flipped through the pages.

"Ah, so you can draw. I thought for a moment that

mayhap you made all that up simply so you could watch me bathe," he said, handing back the sketchbook.

She pushed him away, but there was little point in doing so. Like the oak behind them, he was immovable and pinned to the spot. That her hand touched his naked flesh was also something she ought not to have done. For now, she knew what his skin felt like, hot and hard, and they were two words her mind never needed to seat together.

"You ought to remember your place, Mr. Everett," she reminded him, narrowing her eyes and hoping he understood her ire.

He leaned toward her, almost nose to nose. This close, she could smell his skin. She wasn't sure what he had smelled like before, but right now, he smelled fresh, like summer and man all wrapped into one lovely package of muscular flesh dripping with water and tempting her to see if he tasted as sweet as she thought.

Hailey shook the thought aside. What was she doing thinking such things about a man she had no right considering anything about other than if he were doing his job well and often enough?

"I do apologize, Miss Woodville. I did not mean to insult your sensitive sensibilities. I did not know that you used this part of the river for sketching. I shall not come here again." His lips twitched.

Was he laughing at her? She fisted her hands on her hips as best she could with the sketchbook still in her hold. Annoyance thrummed through her, among other things that she would not admit to.

"You are very outspoken for a stable hand, not to mention you seem to think it's appropriate to speak to me with slights that you assume I do not understand. Well, Mr. Everett, I do understand your tone and words, and I do not appreciate them. If you wish to keep your employment here, you will bathe in the part of the river used by our staff on the occasion that they do not use a hip bath. You shall not accuse me of watching you like a cockish wench. Do you understand me?"

His eyes widened, and he crossed his arms. The muscles on his chest flexed and distracted her a moment. He was so tall and handsome; it was beyond irksome. "You were watching me, Miss Woodville. You may call me a lot of things, but a liar I am not."

His voice, cultured and well-spoken, drawled his reply. There was little doubt he had some form of education. Pity they did not teach him to speak better toward his employers.

"I was not watching you by choice, I assure you," she said, heat rushing to her cheeks, knowing too well that she had been watching him, drinking in every little nuance of his person, wondering what it would be like to be wrapped in arms as strong as his. She really needed to marry and soon. It was long past time she found a husband.

Hailey swallowed.

He grinned, and the breath in her lungs froze. The worst was when that grin morphed into a smile. A very knowing, amused smile, and Hailey knew that no matter what she told herself, he comprehended she had been gawking at him and hoping he would not notice.

"I shall leave you now, but before I go, I will state that no one ought to deny themselves the truth. You were watching me and enjoying what you saw. If you ever wish to see it again, I'll be in the other bathing area used by your staff." With one final grin, he strode off up the small, worn path toward the stables.

Hailey watched him until he was out of sight, remembering to close her gaping mouth before she swallowed a bug. The man was a nuisance and too smart for his own good. Mayhap that was why he was up north in Northamptonshire. There was no one farther south who would hire him.

FIVE

The following day Greyson found himself out in the fields, walking through the barley crops that were almost ready for harvest. The older man explained the crop, what they looked for that told them when it was ready for cutting. The man who went by the name of Bob was gray-haired and looked more in need of retirement than another season of cutting down crops under the summer sun.

Greyson knew, of course, the basics of farming due to the fact he was the heir to several properties hundreds of times larger than the modest Woodville Estate. Even so, he listened to the chap, not wanting to lose this position, no matter how close he may have come to doing just that yesterday with Miss Woodville.

He shook the thought of her aside, not needing to remember the image of her biting her lip as she watched him bathe in the river. Or the reaction his cock had to that very fact.

"Do you know how to use a sickle?" Bob asked him,

handing him the deadly-looking device he'd only ever viewed from afar.

"A little. Would you mind showing me?" he asked, hoping he wouldn't be dismissed on the spot for being such a useless stable hand, and now laborer in the fields. He ought to know these things in the position he was in. But as a marquess and future duke, he knew none of it.

He frowned at the truth of his thought. He ought to learn, even if that learning only improved his understanding of farming and possibly helped his tenant farmers in years to come.

Greyson wasn't even sure if his father bothered with the tenants much at all, other than ensuring they did their job and did it well.

"Hold the sickle here and here," Bob said, demonstrating. "And ye make sweeping cuts low on the crop. Almost to the base of the stem. Watch out for others about ye, mind. The sickle is deadly sharp, and I do not want to see anyone limbless after a day in the field."

Greyson cringed but nodded. Not wanting to see that himself. "May I practice? We will be harvesting soon, will we not?"

"Aye, practice over near the wood. There is some long grass that will work just as well as the crop. See how you go."

Greyson started for the grassy area before the woodland began, where the crop was not planted, and tried his hand at cutting the grass. After a few attempts, he managed to cut the grass to a standard he was happy with, certain he would handle the cutting of the crop well enough.

His valet walked toward him from the direction of the stable. "Everett, you're required back in the stable. Apparently, we cleaned out the stalls so well yesterday that we're honored with doing it again today."

Greyson returned the sickle to Bob and started back to the stables, cursing his father under his breath. "Remind me when I'm the duke to never be such an arse to my son."

Thompson chuckled. "So you will marry and beget an heir. Anyone in mind?" he teased.

"No one as yet," he snapped, thinking of his father's choice. He shuddered at the horror of it all. Lady Francesca may want a union with him, but he certainly did not. He wanted to desire his wife, if not love her, and he did not find the Earl of Lincoln's daughter attractive in any way.

"Still in a mood, Everett? You came back from the river last night in one as well. Care to tell me what happened? One of the other stable hands said they spotted you talking to Miss Woodville."

So he was already the house gossip. Could his time here in Northamptonshire get any worse? "She told me I was bathing in an area she uses for drawing. But I caught her watching me first and teased her about it."

"You did not," Thompson choked before he laughed. "I bet she did not like that. No woman of quality would."

He supposed even if she were only gentry and not noble, Miss Woodville fell under that category of quality. "She did not like it at all. Turned as red as the roses that grow on the north wall of the manor house." He laughed and came around the corner near the stable and slammed directly into the woman herself. She flayed backward, and before he could think not to, Greyson caught her, hoisting her back on her feet.

She did not thank him for his efforts, merely pushed his arms away from her waist and crossed them at her front. An annoyed scowl settled on her face and one that Greyson was starting to think was a permanent feature. At least when he was around.

"My face, Mr. Everett, did not turn as red as the climbing roses, and I insist you apologize before I have you pack your things and leave."

He bowed, schooling his features, the word blue-stocking reverberating about in his mind, not to mention how lovely she felt in his arms, all feminine curves he'd not had the pleasure of for some days now.

"Apologies, Miss Woodville. I only meant that you were as pretty as a rose."

She huffed out a disgruntled breath, and Thompson shook his head as if to warn him to stop talking. He was a marquess and a future duke. There were few times he ever stopped speaking unless *he* wanted to.

"You are a liar, sir." She stepped toward him. "Please leave, Mr. Thompson," she said, not moving an inch. "I would like a word with Mr. Everett."

This close, Greyson could see that her sweet, perfectly proportioned nose came up to his chin. She was a nice height, and should he kiss her, he would not have to stoop too far to get the job done.

Would she kiss him back? He studied her features, her lips drawn tight in annoyance were still full and luscious. Her eyes, as green as the valleys around them, sparkled with ire. Perhaps this time, he had pushed her too far?

"You cannot speak to me in that way. I do not care if you have an opinion on my person. I could do the same to you, but it would not make it right."

"Really?" he asked, leaning against the stable, intrigued. "How would you describe me if you could?"

She glanced around the yard, ensuring they were alone, before coming closer. "I would explain you as a man who does not know how to do a lot of things and needs guidance —a man who has high opinions of himself but very little skills. You are a man without substance, Mr. Everett. Except for perhaps pompous ones. I think you suit that word very well."

Greyson was not pompous. How dare she state such a heinous thing? He was trying hard here, working and doing all that was asked of him. That he did not know as much as the other men was not his fault. He had never been taught. With his status in the Derby dukedom, the heir, there were many things that he did not know. There was nothing wrong with that. But pompous. Oh no, he drew the line at being called such a slur.

"I have more substance than you are aware, Miss Woodville. You are wrong to term me as such."

"I speak as I find, which I'm now certain you do as well. If you have an issue with the way I communicate to you, I suggest you check yourself before saying anything to my face. Or your friend, as I just found."

"That was a private conversation not meant for your ears." Damn, she was pretty when she was annoyed. Her cheeks flushed with color, and her eyes all but glowed with annoyance. This woman was a worthy comrade and one he enjoyed sparring with.

"And yet, I heard them."

"You did not answer my question in truth, though, now did you?" he teased, liking the fact that he was walking along a ledge and certain that any moment she would push him off and free him from this hell on earth. "Pompous is an explanation of one's character, but I'm interested in what you see of me."

She raised her brow, her mouth gaping in the most delicious way. "Do you mean regarding your looks?"

He nodded, more than ready to hear her answer.

"Well," she stuttered, before taking a calming breath, her eyes narrowing in on him once more. "You are a handsome man, I will not state otherwise, for it would be a lie. But that you are more than aware of the fact makes you unappealing to the opposite sex." A small, sly smile crossed her lips. "Happy now, Mr. Everett?"

Unappealing... What on earth was the woman saying. Never had any woman of any rank ever stated he was both pompous and unappealing merely because he was confident in himself.

You can be arrogant and an arse at the same time, Greyson.

He ground his teeth, ignoring the warning voice in his head. "I appreciate your honesty, Miss Woodville, no matter how wrong it is. Good day to you," he said, stepping past her and heading for the stable. He heard her gasp at his abrupt end to their conversation, but better that than he stoop to the level of his pride and tell Miss Woodville that he ought to put her over his knee and show her who was more superior. One day, he promised himself, but that day was not today.

To teach her a lesson required him keeping his job and smacking her arse now would not gain him that.

CHAPTER
SIX

Hailey stormed into the room she shared with her younger sister, Isla, and found her lying on her bed reading.

She unbuttoned her spencer and threw it over the chair before her desk. She leaned on the back of the cushioned seat, staring out at the grounds of the estate, the blood pumping fast in her veins.

How dare he speak to her in such a way? He was laughing at her, she knew it, and he would not get away with it. She ought to storm downstairs to her father and demand he allow her to dismiss the pompous, handsome arse and kick said bottom all the way back to London.

Who had ever heard of a stable hand coming from London in any case? It was any wonder he was so utterly inept with his employment.

"Are you going to tell me what has all your feathers lifted as if you've seen a fox in the hen pen?" Isla asked, laying down her book and sitting up.

Just a year younger, her sister was delicate and pretty and preferred to read rather than take part in running the estate—a smart choice considering who Hailey had to deal with at the moment.

"It is nothing really. A new laborer from London who is less than ideal," she said, going over to her washbasin and pouring water into the bowl.

"Oh yes, I have seen him. Julia mentioned him yesterday, that she had seen him in the stables when she went for a ride. She mentioned that for a stable hand, he was very handsome."

Too handsome if Hailey was to have an opinion on it. And arrogant and too smart with his words. He ought to do his work and certainly not poke fun at her whenever the opportunity arose. What type of person did such a thing?

"Twice now, I have had words with the man. He bathes where I sketch. He dared to accuse me of ogling him when I came upon him in the river. Can you believe it?" Hailey said, throwing her arms up in the air for good measure.

Her sister grinned at her, and Hailey narrowed her eyes. "You do not think his accusations were warranted, do you?"

Isla shrugged, the grin not leaving her lips. "The high color of your cheeks is certainly making me think that you were watching him before he accused you of the fact." Isla patted the bed, and Hailey went to her, sitting at the end of the mattress. "Did he have his shirt on when you saw him?"

Hailey shushed her sister, but even she knew she could not lie. Not to Isla. "He did not. He did, however, have his breeches still on, thankfully, but I did happen to see quite a lot before he spied me."

"So you were watching him." Isla laughed, her eyes sparkling with eagerness. "Tell me more. You know I long for such high adventures like the ones I read in my books."

Hailey spied the book, *The Delusions of the Heart* written by Anne Burke laying on Isla's bed. "Very well, I shall tell you, but you cannot say anything to anyone. I told Mr. Everett that he was mistaken in what he accused me. Even though he was entirely correct in his assumptions."

"You are wicked, Hailey. But do tell me what you saw."

"Well, as for that," she said, remembering the water cascading down his chest and abdomen. The muscular shoulders and stomach, the bronze skin that was sun-kissed and firm. She licked her lips at the very thought of his person. "He was just as fine under his shirt as he is in it. A fine specimen of a man. It is a pity that his mind has nothing but feathers in it, and he's unable to take anything seriously."

"And a face of an Adonis. He is stunning, and unlike any workers we've ever had before. Do you think a man such as he would be a laborer? He seems too fine for manual work. Maybe he's a gentleman's son who's lost his fortune and must make his own way in the world but has not lost his airs and graces that were brought up in him."

Hailey laughed. Her sister's fanciful imaginings too much, even for Mr. Everett. "He speaks better than the servants. Even Mr. Oak could learn a thing or two from his vocabulary, but that may be because they're from London. Perhaps they were footmen in a nobleman's house before heading north for work. I suppose we shall never know for sure, not unless we asked them, and I shall certainly not enter into any more conversations with Mr. Everett if I do not have to."

"I suppose there is little point in being anything but courteous toward him. It's not as if you can look at such a man for marriage. Mama has grand plans for us all, and you most of any of us."

That was very true. She was supposed to have a season in town next year if she did not secure a husband beforehand. Not that she thought such a thing would occur, but the town ball was to be held in two weeks, and it was a good opportunity to practice her dancing and mingle with people she did not know.

"What do you think of Mr. Bagshaw?" Hailey asked her sister. "Do you believe Mama would agree that he is a suitable gentleman who could court me? I know that he is interested. He stated as much last year at the dance in Grafton."

Isla snorted. "I doubt old Martin Bagshaw will be acceptable to Mama, even if he is rich. He's not titled. You know she has her heart set on all of us gaining some sort of lofty form of address that starts with Lady or Her Grace."

"Martin is perfectly acceptable, and it would enable me to remain close to home should Papa need help with the estate. You know how he loves his birds, and I would hate to marry and leave him, and he not have as much time to commit to his hobby."

"I think Papa needs to give up his hobby so that it will enable you to live a life worth living. You cannot remain near our parents and put your own future happiness at risk. You would not be well matched to Martin, he's too old, almost forty, and you are one and twenty. He's almost old enough to be our father."

Isla made a gagging expression, and Hailey sighed. "Well, it was just a thought. I am looking forward to London, do not get me wrong, but a gentleman nearby would be preferable."

"Well, maybe you will find one in London who is from Northamptonshire or another county nearby. Simply do not fall in love with one who is not."

Hailey shook her head at her sister's advice. "Easier said than done, I would assume. That's if I find a love match at all. I may not be courted all season, and then I shall be back here, and my only option will be Martin and no one else. If that does occur, promise me you will still visit me. That you will not stay away simply because he is who he is."

"Of course not," Isla said, reaching for her hand. "I would never treat you with such disrespect. But I will also not allow you to marry Mr. Martin Bagshaw. You will marry a man whom you love and who loves you. I will not settle for less."

Hailey smiled before the image of Mr. Everett flittered through her mind. The man was a menace, even intruding on her good thoughts. She would have to keep him busy and away from her if she were to survive his employment here. That was all there was to it—infuriating popinjay.

SEVEN

Greyson was determined to be better behaved. He could not afford to lose his position here. He would not allow his father the gloating right that he had not lasted three days.

He stood beside a chestnut mare of fifteen hands and saddled the placid mount for Miss Woodville. He would also not ignite the fire that burned in her that he seemed to flame every time they were near each other.

Greyson bit back a smile at knowing he would see her soon. For some foolish, illogical reason, he enjoyed sparring with the woman. Not that he should. She could have him dismissed tomorrow if he read the lay of the house well.

The evening before, he had taken his supper in the kitchens, and the cook was only too willing to tell the tales of the household. It made Greyson wonder if his own staff spoke about the goings-on above stairs as these servants seemed to do. A little mortifying to think such a thing, and he had decided he would prefer not to know.

The sound of Miss Woodville's voice floated toward

him, and patting the mare, he led the docile mount outside the stable toward the hitching block.

"Miss Woodville," he said, dipping his cap and showing her more respect than he had since the moment they had met. "Good morning to you."

Her piercing green eyes narrowed on him, and he knew she was trying to figure out what he was up to. What smart comment was to next come out of his mouth.

"Mr. Everett. Pleasure as always."

He schooled his features, forcing himself not to smile at her double meaning in greeting.

"I have your horse ready for you. Would you like me to help you mount?" he asked.

She nodded, stepping to the side of the horse. "If you could. I prefer not to use the mounting block. Winnie does not like it," she explained.

Greyson set the reins over the mare's neck and handed them to Miss Woodville. Her gloved fingers brushed his uncovered ones, and fire rushed through his blood. She snatched them from him and clasped the horse's reins and saddle in preparation to mount.

Greyson ignored the feeling that coursed through him and gripped her boot, hoisting her up on the saddle. She set her feet in the stirrups and proceeded to ignore him.

"Do you need a groom to accompany you?" he asked, hoping she would say yes, but knowing already that she would refuse.

"No, thank you. I know my way around the estate well enough not to get lost."

He nodded and stepped back. "Enjoy your ride, Miss Woodville," he said, enjoying the sight of her as she trotted out of the yard, her pert, sweet arse lifting every so often.

Her riding habit was tighter than it ought to have been

and hugged her figure, accentuating every delicious curve of her person. He supposed if she were to have a season in town next year, the riding habit would be soon replaced with a more fashionable one. Pity, though, since that one looked so fine on her person.

"Stop drooling, Everett, or it will not only be me who has noticed that Miss Woodville has you in a spin."

"Do not be absurd, Thompson. I couldn't care less about the chit," he spat, returning to the stable and entering Winnie's stall, fixing her hay and filling her water.

"Really," his valet remarked, his tone disbelieving. "You could have fooled me. I have never seen a woman get under your nerves quite so quickly and one who has less than zero interest in you."

"If she knew who I really was, she would be all sweet smiles and giggling laughs at my side, and you know it."

Thompson burst out laughing, wiping his eyes for good measure. "I think not. I could not see Miss Woodville giggling about anything."

Greyson smirked, knowing he could make her giggle if he had a moment alone with her. And not just giggle...

"I see that you have decided to be the obliging stable hand and laborer after all. How long will you be able to withstand such a farce?"

"Long enough to prove my father wrong, and in any case, it is not so bad working for a living. The food is good, and there are no obligations or expectations to meet. It's quite liberating, really."

"Indeed," Thompson stated. "Well, I've been charged with having you ride out on the eastern boundary. If you follow the river, you will meet up with some of the tenant farmers working there. They're building a stone wall to keep the sheep penned during the winter months and need more hands."

"Are you going to help?" Greyson asked, happy that Winnie's stall was ready for the mare when she returned.

"No, I'm to stay and shovel more shit. Unless you wish to swap jobs?" Thompson suggested.

Greyson shook his head. "No, I shall ride out now. Enjoy the excrement," he said, chuckling at Thompson's mumbled insult on his way out.

He saddled and rode out along the river as ordered, taking the time to enjoy the fresh air and dappled light from the woodland that ran along the river. This country-side was very pretty, rolling hills and small farms and cottages scattered about. He had never traveled this far north before, not even to Viscount Billington, who lived near York, but that would change from today. After being here in this county, he realized there was more to England than just London, and he ought to see the country of his birth.

Up ahead, he spied the workers building a stone fence in a rectangular shape that would pen the sheep. It was larger than he thought it would be, and it would be back-breaking work to complete it before winter.

He pulled his mount to a halt and let it graze. He rolled up his sleeves, accepting of the manual work. He had hated it at first, but the more he worked, the more he realized that no estate ran at all without the people in the stables or working the gardens and land.

He had taken a lot for granted, and mayhap Miss Woodville had been somewhat correct in calling him pompous.

"Ah, Greyson, glad you are here. There is a rock quarry just down the hill. If ye could start wheeling them up in the small cart attached to the horse, that would help. We will continue building the wall with what we have already."

"Righto," he said to the foreman, Bob. Another thing he was getting used to, calling people by their first names and not titles. Of course, he knew all of his friend's given names, but they were not used often, if at all. To call a man Bob still did not flow easily off his tongue as Your Grace or my lord.

He took the cart horse's reins and started down the hill. The quarry was small, more like a pile of rocks that looked like they had been dropped and broken in one particular location.

He loaded several, not wanting to make the cart too heavy for the horse to pull uphill, and started back. He continued to do such loads as the day wore on. Sweat beaded his skin, and the sun, warm in the afternoon, beat down on his arms. He would be burned, he was sure.

With another cart of rocks, he crested the small hill and spied Miss Woodville standing near Bob, discussing the yard that the men had made good progress on.

Greyson came to where he was dropping the stones, unloading them, and paused, wiping his brow. He glanced over to where Miss Woodville stood and found her watching him.

Heat licked his skin, and he knew it was not only the sun that warmed his blood. The woman, for some unbeknownst reason, drew him in. She infuriated him as much as she intrigued him.

Not that he could ever look at a woman such as her. His father would never allow such a lowly marriage for his only son. He would cause untold trouble to the Woodvilles simply because of Greyson's interest, and no matter how vexing Miss Woodville was, none of them deserved the wrath of the duke.

He turned his back to her, returning to his work, but even so, he could feel her eyes on him like a physical touch. He could never regard her as an option as a wife, a future duchess, no matter if the wild side of him wondered at it.

At the river yesterday, he had wanted her to touch him, to reach out and lay her hand on his chest. His body had burned with a need to see her bright-green eyes shimmer with need.

Greyson cleared his throat, pushing the inappropriate thoughts aside as he pulled the cart down the hill once more. He needed to get a hold of his urges and wayward thoughts. It was any wonder his father had sent him away. Maybe he *was* incorrigible.

CHAPTER
EIGHT

ailey could not tear her eyes from Mr. Everett, even if her words to the foreman continued to spill from her mouth. Words on how well the build was going and how much they had achieved already today. Her eyes could not shift from Mr. Everett's tanned, sweating arms. Arms that flexed and strained as he lifted rock after rock from the cart to the pile the men took from.

She seized a calming breath, hoping the blush on her cheeks would be mistaken for the warmth of the day and not the inappropriate thoughts that swam through her mind. Thoughts that had not stopped since she had seen him bathe the day before in the river.

"In this part of the hill where it drops into a natural-forming protected gutter, the yard is perfect for the sheep that remain in these parts of the estate during winter."

"The idea was a worthy one, Miss Woodville," her foreman stated, wiping his brow. "We'll make a thatch roof, nothing too spectacular, but it'll do the job well enough."

"That will complete it perfectly," she said. "I brought you all some lunch and some iced tea that I know you all enjoy so much." Hailey returned to her horse and, untying the basket from the saddle, placed it down on a portion of the wall where the men were not working.

"Thank you, Miss Woodville," the men said, their eyes lighting up at the sight of the basket.

"There is ham and cheese, and Cook has a newly baked bread loaf in there for you all. And, of course, some fruit from the orchard. We do not want you all to suffer out here when we know you are all working so hard."

The men smiled and started to move over to a tree where there was plenty of shade for them all to eat. Hailey joined them, sitting on an exposed root to save her dress from the dirt. She took a bread roll from Bob and glanced up in surprise when Mr. Everett sat beside her, ham and a boiled egg in one hand and a bread roll in the other.

"I do not believe I've ever seen a lady of the house have luncheon with her servants, nevertheless their field workers."

She swallowed her bread and thought over Mr. Everett's question. "The houses you worked for before ours, I assume, were higher in status than our own. My father brought us all up to not think of ourselves as any better or less than anyone high born or not."

"And yet you stated to me that I ought to know better how to talk to you, my master."

Heat kissed her cheeks, as she remembered her words, followed closely by shame. "Well, you irritated me with your high-handedness and arrogant speech, and I forgot myself for a moment, but I do not think that, not typically."

"Only when you're around me then?" he asked, a small smirk on his lips.

Hailey tried to bite back a smile and failed miserably. "Yes, only when I'm around you, and you're being too free with your words."

"I've been trying to change my ways since our last interaction. Have you not noticed that I have been on my best behavior since our discussion yesterday? Admit it, you have not heard me once mention your beauty, have you?"

Pleasure coursed through her blood at his words. Beauty? She had never heard such a thing from a man, and yesterday at the stable, she had not thought he truly meant a word he was saying. She had thought he was teasing her, making fun of her in some way, but perhaps he was not.

"Even if we are starting new, Mr. Everett, I cannot allow you to comment on my appearance. That would be inappropriate considering I am unmarried, as are you, and we are not courting."

"You could not court me even if I wished that to be the case. Like most parents, I assume yours wish for you to make a great match in London. I heard you were to London next year for a season?"

Hailey shook her head at the inappropriateness of their conversation, but nor did she wish to put a stop to it. "I am for London next year, and you are right, like most parents, mine wish for me to marry well. I think they would be very well pleased if I married a gentleman of similar status as Papa or a baron if I were so fortunate, but so long as my husband loves me as much as I love him, that is all that I want."

"An honorable way to look at it. I do hope that your season is successful and you gain all that your heart desires."

"Thank you," she stated, studying him as he finished his ham. "And what about you, Mr. Everett? Are you not looking for that special lady in your life? One to settle down with and have children? Or are you too free a spirit to stay in one place too long?"

"I'm no free spirit. If one thing is true about me, that would be it," he declared, his eyes clouding with a sadness she could not understand before he blinked and it was gone.

"Sometimes, I do not think I shall ever marry, but then, like your parents, my father too wishes for grandchildren, and so mayhap I shall have to one day find a wife."

"You make it sound all so formal and unfeeling. I pity your wife if you do not really want her," she said, wishing she could take the words back the moment she said them. "I'm sorry. My mouth has a way of saying things that perhaps not everyone wishes to hear. I'm the oldest, you see, and I am a little forward and bossy and speak my mind more than I ought."

"Do not ever stop stating the truth just to please others. I like that about you," he said, his eyes holding hers longer than proper.

For the life of her, Hailey could not look away. She could lose herself in his large, stormy-blue eyes. He had the longest lashes, too, not that she had noticed them before. There were many things about Mr. Everett that she seemed more aware of now than she had when first meeting him.

Like how his voice, deep and smooth, wrapped about her like a warm embrace when it was not vexing her. That there was no sign of a cockney accent or the hard life she assumed he grew up living.

"Where did you grow up, Mr. Everett? Where is your father?" she asked, not able to place his accent at all.

"My father resides in London. He works for a duke," he stated, matter-of-fact.

Hailey could hardly believe it. Perhaps that was why he sounded so educated. If he lived in a ducal household, he would have had some education.

"A ducal estate. That is impressive. And you lived there with him?"

"I did, but now I have lodgings of my own. But I grew up in Kent before moving to London."

Ah, so that would explain why he did not sound so rough and hard-worn. His childhood had been mostly spent in the country. "I have never been that far south, but I believe Kent to be a lovely county."

"It is one of the prettiest, but Northamptonshire also has its positives, I find," he said, his eyes taking in her every feature.

Hailey swallowed, hoping she would not blush yet again at his intense inspection of her. "When I'm married, I'm hoping to travel about England, see more of the country than just my home county."

"You will not miss your home when you're settled elsewhere?" he asked her, biting the boiled egg in half.

"I was hoping for a match close to home so I may continue helping Father with the estate, but I'm not certain that is possible." Why she was telling him all this, having this personal conversation with a man only yesterday she was determined to loathe forever, was beyond her. But today, he seemed different, open, and willing to be a friend. If a stable hand could be friends with a lady of the house.

He nodded, looking out over the hills, digesting both his food and her words. "There are many gentlemen in London who come from all corners of our great country. I'm certain that you could find one who lives nearby." He paused. "May I ask why it is that your father does not tend to a lot of the farm work that you seem to do so willingly?"

Hailey shrugged, having had this question from her best friend Lila York, who lived just outside Grafton, and just as she struggled to answer Lila, she knew she would fumble with her words to Mr. Everett. "My father, although a gentleman and proud of his home and farm, prefers the company of his birds than those of his workers, or any society for that matter. He will not travel with Mama and me next year to London. It will only be the two of us, but we prefer it that way. Society and crowds only make Papa nervous, and it is better that he remains home where he is comfortable."

"We shall miss you when you leave for London, Miss Woodville," he said, his voice deep and smooth like whisky. As intoxicating as that drink, too, if she were being honest with herself.

"You will miss me scolding you and telling you to mind your manners and be more respectful to your betters, Mr. Everett?"

He threw back his head and laughed. Hailey could not hold back her amusement and laughed with him.

He sobered, catching her gaze, mischief twinkling in his eyes. "I think I shall miss that side of you most of all. I do not think I've ever met a woman such as yourself before. You are quite a wonder, Miss Woodville, but a delightful one at that."

The conversation was utterly inappropriate, and she needed it to end. Hailey stood, dusting down her dress. "Well, I have not left yet, Mr. Everett. Plenty of time for us to quarrel yet again if you enjoy it so much."

He grinned devilishly. "I look forward to it," he quipped.

Hailey walked toward her horse, picking up the picnic basket on her way. Silly little dimwit that she was, just like

Mr. Everett, she looked forward to their sparring as well. And the thought of what tomorrow would bring when she would see him again coursed anticipation through her blood, more than any thought of London and what The Season would bring.

CHAPTER
NINE

The following day Greyson worked to unload a cart of bagged grain stored in the stables for the horses when the sound of a carriage on the gravel drive caught his attention. He stood beside the cart and watched as a black, highly polished carriage rolled to a halt before the house, and a gentleman stepped down shortly thereafter.

The front door opened, and he caught his breath at the sight of Miss Woodville coming to greet their guest, the smile on her face warm and welcoming, so too the bussing of cheeks that she welcomed from him.

He frowned, ignored Thompson, who told him to keep working and instead watched the interaction between the two. They were close, friends perhaps, or maybe more. He studied the man, older than himself by a good decade, he would guess. Not to mention his hairline was receding and made him appear older than mayhap he was.

"Do you know who that is?" he asked Thompson, unsure why the presence of a man on familiar terms with

Miss Woodville would make the hair at the back of his neck stand on end.

But it did, and he did not like the sensation.

"I heard Morris tell two young stable hands to expect him. Ah," Thompson paused, pointing, "there they are now to assist the driver to bring the carriage around to the stables, maybe ask when they get here."

"So he's a family friend from the village or London, do you suppose?"

"Ask the lads now," Thompson said, going back to work. Greyson moved over to where the boys grabbed buckets to water the horses.

He flicked his chin in the direction of the visitor and Miss Woodville. "Who has arrived?" he asked them.

The oldest lad of the two came to stand beside him. "He's a Mr. Martin Bagshaw. Lives just out of Grafton, rich from all accounts but not titled."

At least Greyson had that on the man, not that he could tell Miss Woodville such a thing, but it made him feel a little better. "They seem quite the pair."

"I do not know much more than that." The young lad shrugged. "You'll have to ask Miss Woodville herself if you want to know more."

He supposed he would have to. He watched them laugh and talk as they walked into the house. The sight of her being the sole attention of another man left him on edge. Why he could not explain, she wasn't the kind of woman he normally courted, nor was she of his status. The upper echelons of the *ton* would eat a gentleman's daughter alive should he make her his duchess. Not that his father would allow such a lowly marriage.

The duke wanted him to marry a woman who looked like

a horse. He sighed. Even so, no matter all the difficulties that separated them, Greyson could imagine a union between them. She was strong, kind, and fair, and she had a tongue that was as sharp as a razor, especially when aimed at him.

He liked that about her most of all. She took no tomfoolery from him.

She turned at the door as Mr. Whatshisname entered the house and met his gaze across the yard. As quick as it was, his body burned at the sight of her knowing smile. It hit him directly in the chest and lower still.

Damn it all to hell.

"Watch yourself, Everett. We're not here for you to court the lady of the house," Thompson warned him.

"I would never and nor would she. She believes me to be a servant. A farmhand," he reminded his valet.

"I'm sure if she knew the truth, that would change," Thompson stated, throwing another bag of grain over his shoulder.

Greyson did the same, starting into the stable. "I would trust her true feelings more if she were to welcome my advances in the guise that I'm in now. At least then I would know that she was interested in me and not the title that I come with."

"True, but then you risk putting her offside by lying to her. She will not think you trust her. That you see her as a grubby little fortune hunter that you've so far been able to avoid in society."

All true, and one of the reasons why he had taken on a mistress. The fact he could pay for his pleasure and one that was available to him whenever he wanted was similar to marriage but without the suspicion of marrying someone who did not care for him, the man behind the title, but only the title itself.

His parents' marriage had been loveless, and he did not want that for himself. He may not ever love his wife, but respect and desire would be favorable.

In London, he had been known as a player, a rake, and if that alone did not push Miss Woodville away, the knowledge that he was here, acting a farmhand, a servant, certainly would. She would think of him playing this part as some sort of lark, a way of laughing at them all. He doubted she would like to be seen as a fool, even though his being here was utterly his father's fault. Not his.

Hailey led Martin into the drawing room where her parents welcomed him. As usual, her mother took much more interest in the man than her papa, who sat reading a book on English varieties of birds.

She studied Martin as he sat. His ease with her family and kind eyes had always drawn her toward him, but it had always been a friendship more than anything else. No matter how much she knew he wished for more, his direct gazes that held a little longer than proper or a touch here and there always told of a man who would like to have more than friendship.

She inwardly sighed, wishing he had sparked some kind of romantic reaction within her. He was rich, a gentleman, with large holdings. His home was one of the finest in the county and near to this estate. It was a shame her heart did not jump at the sight of him.

Your heart leaps at the sight of Mr. Everett, and you cannot marry him.

The truth struck her hard, and she pushed the unwelcome thought aside. Mr. Everett was a farmhand, a worker, who thought too highly of his own opinions, even if he had his moments where he was quite pleasant to talk to.

Not to mention deadly handsome.

Mr. Bagshaw cleared his throat. "Who is excited about the Grafton ball? I know I, for one, cannot contain my excitement."

Her mother's eyes lit up at the mention of it. A night of revelry the whole town and county were looking forward to. "Hailey is looking forward to it more than most. As you know, Mr. Bagshaw, we're to London next year for a season, and Hailey will debut. This dance will help her practice and be as perfect as all the other young ladies making their curtsy to the queen."

"Of course," Martin stated, his eyes warming as they took Hailey in. "Miss Woodville will be the picture of grace and beauty and will make Northamptonshire proud with her poise."

A light blush stole across her mother's cheeks, and Hailey schooled her features. Poor Martin, now that she was near him again, her thoughts on marrying the man were nulled. She needed to tell him that she only ever saw him as a friend, and he ought to look elsewhere for a wife. At nine and thirty, her sister stating he was a little too old for her was true. No matter how often people noted that a man in his prime made a much more suitable husband, she was unsure.

The image of Mr. Everett floated through her mind, and she knew to the core of her soul that he was wild at heart. There was something about him that told her so. He would be no easy conquest, nor would he be possibly the best candidate as a husband. He probably had a line of willing maids more than hopeful he would turn his dark-lashed gaze onto them and invite them to take his hand.

She shivered at the thought of such a handsome man wanting her. She wanted to feel her stomach twist in expectation at the sight of her husband. She wanted to shiver as he whispered sweet nothings in her ear. She wanted to be with him, kiss him whenever she wanted. She did not want to feel nothing just as she did right now. Just a pleasant indifference that would not make a happy union.

CHAPTER
TEN

They enjoyed several cups of tea and biscuits that a maid brought in before Mr. Bagshaw sat up with a satisfied grin on his lips. "Should we walk down to the river, Miss Woodville? The day is pleasant, and it will be nice to take the air before I depart," Martin suggested, glancing to the window, a small smile playing about his lips.

"Of course, she would love to, Mr. Bagshaw. Is that not correct, my dear?" her mother answered for her, standing and striding to the terrace door to open it.

Hailey met her mother's excited smile and wondered if she knew something that she did not. Her eagerness put Hailey on guard, and she stood. "Of course, if you wish to, Mr. Bagshaw."

"I shall send Molly with you as a chaperone."

"Thank you," Martin said, holding out his arm. Hailey threw him a small smile before encircling her arm with his. They started onto the terrace and down to the lawn. They followed the small graveled path that led to the lake.

Although this part of the river was very picturesque, it

was not her favorite outlook. The location where she drew her birds, she liked to keep for herself, while her family preferred the outlook from the terrace. One could also swim in this section of the river when the weather was particularly hot.

"Will you allow me to ask for the first dance at the ball, Miss Woodville?" Martin asked her, keeping to formalities, even though in the past he had slipped once or twice when they were alone to use her given name.

Hailey nodded, willing to give him a dance, they were friends after all, and he was a nice man, even if he were a little too old for her. "Of course. I look forward to it," she said, catching sight of Mr. Morris and Mr. Everett leading horses toward the shallow part of the water's edge. She had not seen it this year, but sometimes the horses who liked the cooling water would go down for a swim.

They stood at the side of the river, Mr. Morris and Mr. Everett talking as Mr. Morris allowed his horse to walk in the shallows. Mr. Everett wasn't content to do just that and led his horse farther into the water. She felt a rush of heat to her face when he pulled his shirt from his breeches and up over his head, discarding it onto the grassy banks. Hailey swallowed at his exposed abdomen, the taut muscles that flexed and glistened in the sunlight as he enjoyed the water as much as the horse.

She glanced at Mr. Bagshaw and found his mouth agape, his eyes wide as he took in their farmhand. Hailey's eyes were drawn back to the sight of the half-naked man. Mr. Everett now sat on the back of the chestnut gelding, the horse pawing at the water as if it were about to lie down.

His laughter and smile made her catch her breath. A mixture of emotions thrummed through her. Confusion, excitement, not to mention need, which was more surprising than anything. Whatever would she need from Mr. Everett? His smile and bellowing laughter made her catch her breath. He was as magnificent as his naked chest was.

She bit her lip, knowing that she was ogling the man and unable to stop the madness that floated through her mind that she would like to be the reason for his smile, laughter, and happiness.

"I say, your servants are very uncouth, Miss Woodville. I think you ought to talk to your father about this man. It's most unseemly."

Hailey fought not to grin. She knew very well how unseemly Mr. Everett was being, yet she was also thankful that she had witnessed his nakedness. It was a gift she had not thought to receive.

"I shall speak to him. I'm sure he did not think anyone from the house would be down here while they let the horses play." As if sensing they were talking of him, Mr. Everett glanced toward them, and their eyes met, held. A shock ran through her, and she felt his dark, hooded gaze as if he had physically touched her.

She shivered. She ought to look away. Storm up to him and demand he dress appropriately when in her employment, just as Mr. Bagshaw suggested, but she did not. Could not. To do so would go against everything in her body that, right at that moment, she wanted to memorize forever—his every little nuance. His disheveled hair and his laughing eyes. Oh yes, she wanted to remember this day for the rest of her life.

Gosh, he was handsome.

"It is a shame I find that the ball allows everyone from Grafton to attend," Martin stated, his voice tinged with distaste.

The annual ball, held in the town's main hall, was for everyone who lived and worked in the area to attend and enjoy. It was a night the different classes came together to enjoy an evening of revelry and celebration of the upcoming harvest. This year the harvest is to be one of their best for several years. It will be celebrated more than most.

"Come now, Mr. Bagshaw, do not sound so disappointed. The ball is for everyone to enjoy, as you know very well."

"With men such as the one wading about in the water, I think it is time that rule was changed."

Hailey frowned, fighting not to reply with a biting remark that would certainly upset Martin more than he was already. "You have never had an issue in the past with the ball. What has brought on this change of heart?" she asked, although she had an inkling that part of his ire was the half-naked servant out in the water, playing about like some male water nymph set to seduce any female within sight of him to his side.

Certainly, it would not take much for Hailey to throw away all the rules and wishes of her mother and go to Mr. Everett and let him do what water nymphs did to seduce unsuspecting humans.

Would he kiss her, wrap those strong, muscular arms about her waist and pull her close? What would his muscles feel like under her palms?

She sighed, the image of such a thought teasing her senses.

"I believe that there should be limits to who is in attendance, that is all. I should hope that your male servants are more appropriately dressed than they are now when they arrive."

Hailey pulled away as anger replaced any patience she

had for the man. He really was being a little too prudish, even for her. "You sound like a pompous snob, Mr. Bagshaw. Maybe the ball isn't appropriate for you any longer since it allows such rabble to attend as you think."

Her words seemed to pull Martin from whatever hole of distaste that he had descended into, and he shook himself. "I apologize, Miss Woodville. I did not mean to offend. I simply do not think you should be exposed to such inappropriate behavior, such as the man in the lake. Shall we return to the house? I'm certain your mama will have more refreshments ready by now."

More food and tea? Had the man not eaten before he came to visit? "Of course," she said, turning and starting for the house. She did not wait for him, annoyed that he would chastise her regarding her own servants. Or that he had the audacity to want to disinvite the majority of people in the county due to his snobbishness. His steps quickened on the gravel path behind her, and she did not attempt to speak again even as he tried to converse on the gardens and the congenial weather they had been experiencing of late.

Hailey knew that Mr. Bagshaw had always been a little too high in the instep. But not so much to voice those opinions out loud and about her workers too. It was rude, and he ought to know better.

The sooner she told him they would never suit, the better.

***

Late that evening, Greyson sat in the hay barn, drinking a glass of beer they had been given after the heavy day of unloading grain and looking after the horses. Moonlight streamed into the space from the windows that were up high on the walls, and it was easy to see without a lamp. Not that anyone with half a brain would bring a burning object into a hay storage barn.

The swim in the river was refreshing, and he had enjoyed spending time with Morris, the foreman of the stables, more than he thought he would. The man, much older than himself, was intelligent and no-nonsense, which he preferred in anyone he conversed with.

Not to mention he had invited him and Thompson to dine with him and his wife at their cottage that sat on the outskirts of the property. He had accepted and was looking forward to the evening and the company of people other than those he worked with each day.

The door to the barn opened, and he stilled at the sight of Miss Woodville as she came inside, the moonlight chasing her indoors.

"Mr. Everett," she queried when she spied him sitting on the hay. He stood and dusted himself down before finishing his drink.

"Miss Woodville. I was having a moment of quiet before retiring for the night."

She nodded and came into the building, going over to where the lucerne was stacked and picking up a biscuit. "I was just getting a treat for Winnie. She loves lucerne, and I have not given her any these past days."

He went over to her, reaching up higher on the pile and picking out a bigger biscuit than she had grabbed. "Here, this one is bigger and fresher. Winnie will be more thankful."

She smiled, taking it from him before throwing the one she had onto the pile. "I saw you today, swimming with the horses. You looked as if you were enjoying yourself."

"That is because I was," he admitted, seeing no reason

to admit that the day had been more enjoyable than any he had experienced in a long time. A day of work granted, but good conversation and amusing moments with the horses had made the day sprint by. He could almost admit to looking forward to the next. "I enjoy working with the horses more than anything else."

She met his gaze, and his stomach clenched at the sight of her here with him. They ought not to be. He knew that more than anyone. As a marquess and son of a duke, he ought to be careful of who he was unattended with, but nor could he shift his feet from the wooden floor. They were stuck there for as long as Miss Woodville was in this barn.

"I do too, although Mama frowns upon me doing such things these days. I'm to be a lady if you recall. Ready for London and nothing but proper behavior for the Season ahead."

She said the words with a tinge of distaste, and he wondered if she were looking forward to the trip as much as he thought. "I should think you'll do well in London. You're very beautiful and kind. You will have gentlemen lining up to dance with you, even if the prospect is not so appealing to you right now."

Never had Greyson ever said anything so true, but nor would he apologize for his words. After all, they were the truth, and although they would circulate in different social spheres in London, he knew that she would be a catch. One would have to be blind not to see how marvelous she was.

Just as he had noticed how marvelous she was and how much he wanted to kiss her full lips under the moonlit sky.

CHAPTER
ELEVEN

Hailey's heart thumped hard, and she was sure Mr. Everett could hear the drum reverberating from her body. She clutched the lucerne against her chest, lest she swoon at his feet at the satisfying words he was saying.

Beautiful and kind. Oh, that was too much and yet also not enough. She wanted to hear such words from a man she admired. She liked Mr. Everett very much, his arrogance when they had first met had waned since their lunch together on the hill some days ago, and he was much more palpable to talk with.

He watched her, and she couldn't miss the interest that burned in his gaze. The question that lingered there. The same question she was asking herself right at this moment.

For some absurd, utterly ridiculous reason, she had the overwhelming thought to kiss him. To take life into her own hands and kiss a man before duty and expectations bore down on her next year.

Never had she ever experienced a desire for another as

she did right at this moment, and there lay the rub. What to do about it? How to initiate a kiss in the first place?

He may turn about and tell her to return to the house. To stop such foolery since their social positions were so different and nothing could come of the kiss.

Mr. Everett's blue eyes burned hotter as the silence stretched between them like kindling on a fire. The breath in her lungs hitched, and Hailey could not shift from where she stood. "You shouldn't compliment me so. It's not seemly," she said, her chastisement half-hearted.

He closed the space between them, looming over her. She looked up, shadowed by his very presence that made her feel things she'd never felt before. Expectation, desire, need.

She swallowed, the need the worst of all. After all, she was one and twenty and had never properly kissed a man. Would Mr. Everett be her first?

"It would seem that your guest this afternoon seemed quite enamored of you. I imagine he complimented you often when you walked down by the river."

Hailey took a moment to compose herself at his questioning. He should not be asking her this, yet a small part of her liked that he did. Was he jealous? Had he taken an interest in her guest and did not like him?

She couldn't hold back her grin. "Are you envious of Mr. Bagshaw? He's a gentleman, you know," she mentioned, but unsure really as to the reason why she said such a thing. Mr. Everett did not care if Martin was a gentleman or not or even who he was at all. His appearance, if anything, looked mildly bored at the mention of her only suitor, which she could understand. Martin was a little dull and certainly did not spark an ounce of interest in her.

"A gentleman, is he? A little long in the tooth perhaps

for a woman yet to make her debut in town." He reached out, slipping a stray curl that had escaped her many pins behind her ear. She shivered as his fingers grazed the whorl of her ear. "You cannot tell me that you're interested in him."

"Mr. Bagshaw is certainly who a young woman ought to marry and be happy with her choice. He's polite and kind." Mostly, she wanted to add, unless it involved her servants, and then he was not so charitable. Which, in her opinion, was a failure. "I have little doubt that he will make me an offer, just as a gentleman should if one is courting a woman."

Mr. Everett scoffed. "And you will say yes to this offer? Would you be happy to have years and years ahead of you talking of important nothings and country gossip? I do not think so," he said, his gaze burning into hers.

He studied her a moment, his inspection making her shiver. "You're a beautiful woman with an honest heart, I think. You should be a duchess, not a country gentleman's wife."

She took a calming breath, closing her eyes a moment to remove all sight of him. He was as intoxicating and sweet as champagne and not a person she needed to have inappropriate thoughts about.

He tipped up her jaw, and she opened her eyes, meeting his gaze. "You should not say such things, Mr. Everett."

"I shouldn't say a lot of things, but I do," he said, closing the space between them.

For a moment, Hailey watched as he lowered his head toward her. His lips, full and soft-looking, moved to take hers, but she could not have that. She was a gentleman's daughter and his employer—a lady who should not be going around kissing farmhands. Anything between them was doomed from the very beginning.

She pushed at his chest and bolted toward the exit. She made it as far as the barn double doors before a strong, immovable hand closed about her arm and swung her around. The momentum threw her into his chest and his mouth covered hers.

Hot and demanding swam through her mind before desire clutched at her with its wicked claws. The little denying beast within her shouted to push him away. This was wrong. Against the rules.

Soon she was silenced by his tongue slipping against hers. She gasped through the kiss, her hands clutching at his shirt to keep him near. He took her mouth over and over, his tongue tangling and drawing a response that she was more than willing to give. The stubble of his jaw rasping against her cheeks.

Would he mark her? Would his kisses display to anyone who came into contact with her that he had thoroughly kissed her?

It was heavenly and utterly against the rules, but then, she no longer wanted to live by those rules if it meant he could no longer have her the way he was right now.

She broke the kiss, pushing against his chest. "Stop, we must stop. I don't even know your name," she mumbled, her head spinning.

A small, devilishly handsome grin twisted his lips. "Greyson. My name is Greyson."

His voice, deep and gravelly, pulled at a part of her never before awoken. Greyson... A strong, commanding name, just as the man in her arms was too. "You may call me Hailey if you will allow me to call you by your given name," she said, hoping he would welcome further intimacy between them. Not that she should. Oh, this was all so wicked and wrong.

But the most excitement you've also ever had in your life...

"Kiss me again, Hailey." He moved to take her lips once more.

She pressed a finger to his mouth. He kissed her finger playfully, and the need in her grew. "Should you not wait for my reply, Greyson?"

He growled, taking her hand from his mouth and kissing her again. This was wrong, utterly ruinous, but marvelously wonderful too. Hailey liked the sound of her name on his lips, and she wanted his lips on hers. Whatever would she do now that she had kissed him?

Once would never be enough.

His hands encircled her, pulling her hard against him. She clutched at his shoulders, his height and punishing mouth making her lose all sense of time and decorum. He consumed her. His teasing kisses drew her to give him more of what he solicited. To step into a void of desire, of wants and needs. It was too much.

He was like the sun, and if one moved too close, they would burn to a cinder.

"Hailey, are you in there?" a familiar voice called from outside.

She tumbled out of his arms just as her sister Isla poked her head about the stable door and smiled in relief. "Ah, you are in here. You took forever to get Winnie's treat, and I thought to check everything was well..." Her words trailed off when she noticed Greyson. Her sister's eyes narrowed in suspicion.

Hailey picked up the lucerne that sat at her feet. Winnie's feed long dropped after the kiss she had embarked upon with Greyson had consumed her mind and muddled her completely.

She walked to her sister, taking her arm and turning her toward the door. "Thank you for your assistance, Mr. Everett. I appreciate the help."

"The pleasure was all mine," he said, bowing slightly like a gentleman. She bit back a grin, knowing there was no gentleman at all under that fine layer of skin that encompassed his body. He was a rake, and a very fine kisser, not that she had anything to compare him to, but he certainly seemed to know what he was doing.

"You look decidedly flushed, Hailey," her sister stated, pinning her with a knowing stare.

Hailey attempted mock outrage and knew she was failing miserably. "It's a warm night."

Her sister shook her head. "You lie," Isla stated, pulling her to a stop. "I can see by your face that you are lying to me. Did you kiss Mr. Everett? Please tell me you did, for if you have done something naughty for a change instead of being always so perfect for our parents, I will be well pleased and proud of you."

Hailey looked about, ensuring they were alone. "You cannot say a word. Please do not tell our sisters or even Lila, not at least until I've had a chance to tell her myself. They would not understand."

She was due to visit Lila soon, and she had never kept anything from her best friend since childhood. Lila, her closest friend who lived in Grafton, would understand, and then she would demand that she do it again and again if she liked it so very much.

That wouldn't be a possibility for Hailey, unfortunately. Just like Romeo and Juliet, they were doomed before they even began.

"I will not tell our parents or sisters," Isla said, making a cross against her chest. "But I demand you tell me why it is that I found you in the barn with a farmhand, and moments after he had thoroughly kissed you senseless. Are you courting scandal?"

"No, of course not. It simply just kind of happened." She knew she was rambling. "And you do not know that the kiss made me senseless."

Her sister chuckled knowingly. "Oh yes, I do know that it did. If it were not from your sparkling eyes or red cheeks, or for that matter, well-kissed lips, your muddled hair would have given you away." Isla grinned at her, amusement making her eyes bright.

Hailey thought about the kiss, knowing tonight she would never sleep. Not with the memory of his mouth on hers. That alone would keep her awake for hours. Worse was her longing to do it again. She glanced over her shoulder and found him watching her, his tall frame leaning casually against the barn threshold.

Her stomach somersaulted, and she quickened her pace toward the stables. Nor would sleep come since now that she had kissed him, her mind furiously thought of how and when she could kiss him again.

And how soon she could make that happen.

CHAPTER
TWELVE

"Please prepare my horse, Mr. Everett," Miss Woodville, Hailey as he would forever think of her after last evening, stated with an air of authority. "You will accompany me on my ride today. I'm visiting a friend in Grafton and need an escort."

Greyson tipped his hat, biting back the small grin on his lips as she turned about and left the stable, the scent of roses lingering in her wake. His gaze dipped to her pretty green riding ensemble and the fashionable hat that covered her brown locks.

She looked every bit the lady this morning. Elegant and regal, commanding and damn it all to hell, he wanted to kiss her again. He wanted to tip off her little hat that would offer no shade to the harsh sun, slip his fingers through her locks and take her sweet mouth.

Last evening he had dreamed of her. Had dreamed they had tumbled into the hay in the barn where she found him, rolled about until they were both stripped of their clothing, nothing but flesh on delicious flesh. He had taken her on the soft bed of straw, made her gasp and moan his name as he brought her to climax.

He'd woken up with a hard cock and had promptly removed himself from everyone else's presence, strode to the river, and dived in. Even now, his cock twitched at the sight of her. The sound of her voice, her scent, the thought of doing all the wicked things he wanted to.

Greyson shook his head, going to where her mare Winnie was stalled and led her out. It did not take him long to saddle the mare, who was more than ready for her ride out if her foot-stomping was any indication.

He hitched Winnie to a post, saddled his own mount, and walked both horses from the stables, finding Hailey's arms crossed, glaring in his direction.

"Do you need a leg up?" he asked her, unsure why she was so prickly this morning.

She shook her head, lifting her skirts a little to reveal trews. "No, I'm not riding side-saddle today, but astride. I won't need any assistance," she said, doing as stated. Without help, she placed her boot into the stirrup and lifted herself onto the saddle, making it look easier than he knew it to be.

Greyson quickly followed and had to push his mount into a canter to catch up to Hailey. She did not look at him, not until they were well away from the house.

He didn't like the fact that he was a dirty little secret that she had to keep. No woman of standing would play about with a laborer on their estate, even though he was a marquess and future duke who outranked all of them.

He ground his teeth, wishing he could tell her the truth, but what of it even if he did? He could not marry her. His father would be sure of that. Not to mention his lies would hurt her. He was buggered whichever way he stepped.

"Who is the lady you are visiting in the village, Miss Woodville?" he asked, using her formal name and hoping she would understand that her coolness toward him halted him from using her given name. But he wanted to talk to her, hear her voice and discuss all manner of things.

Surprisingly he wanted to get to know her. Not a trait he was known for in London and toward the opposite sex.

She glanced at him before steering her horse away from a low-lying branch. She was an accomplished rider. "My friend, Miss Lila York. She lives just outside Grafton on another farm."

He wanted to ask her desperately why she needed to see her friend. Did she need to discuss their kiss? Have her friend chastise her not to do it again? Tell her that she had been reckless? All true, of course, but Greyson could not deny that kissing Hailey had been one of the best kisses he had ever had, even if it was only a kiss, and went no further.

"I suppose you have much to discuss," he stated, matter-of-fact.

Hailey pulled her horse to a stop and faced him. "I do. You are right. You seem displeased that I'm going into town. Maybe you would prefer to be working back at my father's estate. You may go back to the stables if you would prefer. It is not so important that I have a companion. I just thought that you would want to be in my company."

He raised his brow, a little confused by her irritable countenance. "Normally, after a kiss such as the one we shared last evening, I would want to be in your company when it is not so frosty as it is now. I cannot help but think you're angry with me for some unbeknownst reason." Or mayhap she was angry with herself. That she had kissed a man beneath her and regretted it.

"I am not angry with anyone," she stated, the scowl between her eyes deepening.

He threw her a disbelieving look. "Really. If you had a mirror and could see yourself right at this moment, I do not think you would even believe your own words."

"Well, you are wrong."

Greyson narrowed his eyes, moving his horse closer to hers. "Are you angry at yourself, Hailey? Angry that I kissed you and a poor farmhand such as myself has made you feel things you've never felt before? Is that why you're so icy toward me today?" He reached out, cupping her cheek. Her skin was soft and warm, and the pit of his stomach clenched.

Damn it, what was it about this woman that made him all at odds with himself? Made him want things with her that he ought not to.

Her hand covered his, and like a bolt of lightning, he felt her touch to the core of his soul. "I did not want anyone to suspect anything had happened between us back at the stables. As much as I wish things could be different, my family would never allow a union between us."

Neither would his. But he kept the words locked away with his secret of who he really was and why he was working on her farm to begin with. Whatever would he do if their paths crossed in London next year and she found out who he really was?

She would be mortified and never forgive him, and he hated the thought of hurting her in that way.

You will hurt her no matter how she finds out the truth.

Greyson pushed the thought aside, not wanting to think of the future but only the here and now. "I understand, I do. But that does not mean when we're alone as we are now, that we cannot enjoy each other's company." He leaned down, brushing his lips against hers. "If only you knew how much you occupied my mind."

"Do I occupy it much?" she asked him, a small smile playing about her lips for the first time that day. He wanted to see more of her smiles. Not of her worrying about things that were out of their control and in the future. Worries not to be concerned about now.

"You were quite a lot. And what pleasant dreams they were," he admitted, kissing her lips again and her cheeks, one by one as the blush on her skin deepened.

Her hands slid over his shoulders to link at his nape. "We're being reckless. What if someone sees us?" she stated, turning to look back from where they had ridden.

"We will worry about that if it happens, but until then, I want you to know that I'm going to kiss you every chance I get, Miss Woodville, and you will allow me to."

She chuckled, the laugh carefree and warm. "Very well, if you insist. But that must work for me too. I am in charge, after all."

"Oh, of course," he agreed, nodding. "I would not want it any other way," he whispered, taking her lips in a searing kiss and showing her in truth who was superior.

CHAPTER THIRTEEN

Hailey pulled back from the kiss, her body alive with excitement and expectation. How could she feel like this after just last evening being in his arms?

But then, that was not necessarily true. From the moment they had met, he had occupied her mind more than anyone ever had in the past. He had a charisma about him that drew the eye, and she knew that something might come to pass between them.

She had thought it might be friendship. She had not expected it to be anything more.

She could not say what that more was right now, but it was wonderful, addicting, and she could not get enough of it.

"Shall we let the horses roam and go sit under the tree over there? I'm not due at Lila's home for another hour or so," she suggested.

Greyson jumped off his horse, loosening the reins of his mount, and came over to help her down. His strong hands settled against her waist, and the breath in her lungs hitched. Her heart thumped a million beats a minute as he guided her to the ground. She slipped against his chest, and heat licked at her skin. The feeling of his hard chest, his hands strong and sure upon her body, made her knees weak.

He let her go as soon as her boots hit the ground, and just as he did with his own horse, he loosened Winnie's reins and let the horses graze before taking her hand and walking her over to the tree.

They sat on the grass beneath the leafy foliage, the dappled light cooling her from the warm day.

"Did you know that I had a bet with Papa about you? I told him that you would not last the month before you returned to London."

He chuckled as he came to lie beside her, leaning on his hand and looking up at her. Hailey leaned back against the trunk of the tree, studying him. He was so handsome, so utterly unlike anyone she had ever met before. Why could he not be a gentleman's son or even a titled gentleman who thought her worthy of his attention?

Had it been so, both their lives would be so much simpler than they are now. She couldn't let her emotions carry her away. She could not become attached. Her heart would suffer if she did.

You are already attached...

She ignored the warning thought and settled her hands in her skirts.

"My first month isn't over yet." He grinned. "But in all truth, why would you bet such a thing?" he asked, a curious frown marring his normally perfect brow.

She took the hand that rested between them, lifting it before her face. "Because of this," she said, running her hands over his palm and fingers, all of which were soft and supple.

"Because of my hand?" He looked more confused than ever, and she laughed.

"No, because I told Papa from the looks of your hands you had not done a full day of laborious work in your life and that doing so at our estate would be too hard."

He laughed, linking his fingers with hers and bringing them to his lips, kissing her. Her stomach twisted, and she fought not to fall in love with the man. He was so cultured, a gentleman who seemed to know a way to a woman's heart.

"I hope that I have proved you wrong and that mayhap you placed your bet on the wrong horse, for I don't have any intention of going anywhere."

Was that because of her? Or simply because he enjoyed working at their estate? She took a calming breath, looking out over her father's land. "I sometimes wish time would stop so that I never had to meet expectations or do what others wish me to do. I wish I could have been like you and left my home, seeking an exciting life. Meeting new people and gaining new interests. Enjoy whatever adventures came my way."

He kept her hand in his, his thumb idly rubbing against hers. "My life is not as carefree as you may believe. My family, like yours, wants me to marry and settle down. And although our station in life is quite vast, I find myself wanting to halt time too so I may lie here with you forever. You are captivating, Miss Woodville, and I do not think I shall ever want to leave."

She smiled down at him, hoping what he said was true and not some fanciful speech he sprouted to every woman he kissed. Was she one of many? Did he have a bevy of lovers or women who wished they had been trailing in his wake?

She hated the idea of such a past.

"Will you stay when I go to London?" she asked, wondering if he would disappear.

He turned to glance out over the land, and she could see her question caused him concern. "I'm uncertain. The truth of my being here is my father has sent me away to work, and when he is no longer angry with me, he will ask me home. He is somewhat strict and the head of our family, and I will have to leave when he demands that I do."

She pulled him up to sit beside her. Now she could see his face more clearly, hopefully, read him better. "Your father sounds quite ominous. I would have thought he would be pleased that you found employment at a gentleman's estate. You have fit in well here, and I know Mr. Oak speaks highly of your toil."

"My father is proud and harsh, and no matter how well that I do, no matter where it is that I am, I know that he would be disappointed. I have always been a disappointment to him."

Hailey hated the man already for making his son feel so low. "Do you have any siblings? Surely you do not have to suffer your father's ill-temper on your own?"

He sighed, running a hand through his hair and leaving it on end. "Unfortunately, it is me who must deal with him."

His hair still stood on end, and Hailey could not stop the small giggle that escaped. She reached up, smoothing it as much as she could with her hand. "Your hair was sticking up," she explained, not wanting him to think she ran her fingers through every man's hair like it was a common occurrence.

His eyes caught hers. He had the darkest blue eyes she had ever seen, and having his full attention made her breath catch. He was so intense and made her want things she should not.

"I like having your hands on me," he admitted, leaning closer.

Hailey wet her lips, words failing her a moment. "You do?" she whispered, letting her hands drop to his shoulders. They were wide, and she remembered what he looked like in the river bathing. The long, strong lines of his back. How his sun-kissed skin glistened in the daylight and made her want to touch those parts of him too.

"I want to kiss you again." His hand cupped her cheek.

Hailey could not wait another moment, and she closed the space between them and kissed him. She felt his smile through the kiss before his tongue teased her lips, and she lost herself to the embrace.

He used the opportunity to kiss her deeply. His tongue tangled with hers, and this time she had some notion of what to do. Fire coursed through her blood, and she kissed him back with all the desire she felt for the man in her arms.

Her body ached in places she had never known, and when his hand slipped down her waist, squeezing beneath her ribs, she adored every second of it. "Touch me, Greyson," she begged him, slipping her arms about his neck.

He pulled back from the kiss, his eyes heavy-lidded with need. "Are you certain?"

He was breathless, and she nodded, wanting his hands on her more than anything in the world. "Yes. Touch me. Please."

The words lingered between them before he made what

sounded like a half-growl, half-moan before kissing her again. His mouth took hers in a punishing kiss, stealing her breath, and she knew she would never be the same after today. Never be the good eldest girl of Mr. and Mrs. Woodville, and that she never wanted to be ever again.

CHAPTER
FOURTEEN

top, Greyson, his mind warned, but no sooner did he have the thought that she kissed him back, her tongue sliding against his, then all common sense dissipated into thin air.

She was marvelous, spirited, and sweet. Her lips tasted of sin and sugary goodness that he wanted to savor, to gorge himself on until he was sated. And yet something told him he would never get his fill of her. That he would always want this woman kissing him back with as much passion as his own.

He was not sure what it was about Hailey that made all sensible thought impossible, and nor would he think about such things right now. Other things, delicious things, occupied his mind. He wrapped his arm around her waist, lifting her to lie down on the bed of grass.

She did not let him go nor stop her wicked kisses. He suckled her tongue, settling beside her, his hand slipping along the soft muslin of her dress. He could feel the slim lines of her body, her soft stomach that tightened when he ran his hand across it.

"You're so beautiful, Hailey." Never had he seen a woman who oozed beauty inside and out as she did. She was strong, capable, and kind, and more people, himself included, ought to be like her.

He felt along the underside of her breasts, and her breath caught. She reached down and covered his hand with hers, shifting him to touch her breast. "Touch me, Greyson, before I expire." She met his eye, and a wicked light burned in hers. He was only too willing to obey her order.

His cock hardened, pushing against his trews. He did as she asked, kneading her breast, circling her nipple with the palm of his hand. It beaded through her gown, and satisfaction ran through him.

She bit her lip, her eyes wide with awakening.

"Do you like that?" he asked, running his finger along the top of her bodice, slipping down her gown with a patience he did not think he possessed.

"Yes." He exposed her breast. Her nipple was indeed beaded, and he could not deny himself a taste of her. He dipped his head, kissing the rosy peak, running his tongue about the areola before taking her fully into his mouth.

"Oh, my, Greyson," she pleaded.

He moaned. She was so responsive. She undulated under his kisses, pushing her breast into his mouth. He savored her, kissed and teased her flesh before pulling the other side of her gown down and taking his fill.

"That feels so good," she said, her fingers spiking through his hair.

Never in his life had he wanted to lift up a woman's skirts, sink himself into her wet, aching flesh and have his way.

He knew she was wet and needy for him, and should he do what he wanted, he had little doubt she would refuse him. But he could not. Not because of who he was but because he could not take her innocence. Not without taking a vow first, and he would never be the one who would have that honor.

However, that did not mean he could not make her come. He wanted to be the first man ever to make her moan, and he wanted his name on her lips when it happened.

He slid his hand over her stomach, ruching up her dress and sliding it up her legs. He wanted to look, to drag himself from her breasts, but thought better of it. To see her legs, her garters, and sweet mons would be too much, and he could break the one rule he had agreed not to fail.

He teased her thighs through her trews, having forgotten she wore them under her dress. He ran his hand on the inside of her thigh, spreading her legs. She moaned, throwing her head back when his hand grazed over her cunny—the dampness of her desire seeping through her trews.

He bit the inside of his mouth, fighting to keep his own needs and desires at bay. He ripped at the buttons keeping him from her sex, slipping his hand inside. She moaned when his fingers teased the slit of her sex, dipping farther to where paradise was found and pushing against her.

She was wet, and he kissed her hard to distract himself from wanting her so much. The kiss was savage and challenging and stole his breath. She kissed him back with as much passion. Her fingers traveled down his back, scoring his skin.

He stroked her cunny, teasing the bead that he knew

longed for his touch. She bucked against his hand when he rubbed it with his thumb. "You like that, my darling?" he asked her.

She covered his hand with hers, pushing him to touch her more. Her legs closed about their hands, holding him captive. "Yes. Yes, I like it."

He swallowed. The sensation that he would spend in his breeches thrummed through him. His balls, tight and hard, lifted, and he knew with the slightest touch he'd come. Hell, he wanted to fuck her. He wanted to slip the buttons free on his breeches, rip hers off and sink into her aching flesh.

"Please, Greyson," she begged him.

He could not deny her. He slipped a finger, then two, into her core. Her wetness covered his fingers, and he moaned, fucking her with his hand. She lifted her derrière, seeking more, and he would give her all that she wanted, all that she needed. With his thumb, he teased her nubbin, and she moaned. He could feel her tighten about his fingers, and he knew she was close.

"Come for me, Hailey. I want to be your first. I need to be your first."

His words must have acted as a catalyst, for wetness coated his hands, and she clutched at his shoulders with a frenzy he'd not seen before. She gasped, clutched at him. He watched her, head thrown back, her eyes closed in bliss as her body shook with her release.

She was the most beautiful woman he'd ever seen in his life.

He wished it were his cock that she rode through the tremors that shook her. He wanted her with a need that scared him. He had never felt like this after sex. And today, he had not even found his release.

But for once, it did not matter. All he cared about was her happiness, her pleasure. Giving her satisfaction on a bed of grass in the wilds of Northamptonshire.

He leaned down, kissing her lips. The kiss, soft and beckoning, pulled her from whatever place she had gone to. She kissed him back, her hands slipping once more about his neck and holding him close.

He broke the kiss, watching her and marveling again at her beauty. "You did not scream my name, Hailey," he teased, sliding his hand against her mons and dragging every last ounce of pleasure from her he could.

"Hmm, really?" she asked, her eyes heavy with satisfaction. She kissed him quickly, her hand grazing across his jaw. "Was I supposed to?"

He nodded, swallowing hard at her wickedness.

"Well then," she continued. "I suppose we shall have to do this again and see if you can make me scream your name the next time."

Oh dear God, the thought of such a thing made his cock twitch, and he couldn't help but press against her leg, taking a little pleasure for himself. "Is that a challenge?" he asked her.

She smiled, rolling him onto his back and coming to lean over him. "Oh yes, Mr. Everett. It most certainly is." She grinned, kissing him again, and he lost himself in her touch, her scent, everything that made her who she was.

Do not tumble for her, Greyson. She's not for you.

He thrust the thought aside, kissing her back, knowing that somewhere, deep inside himself, he knew that to be a lie. That maybe Hailey was exactly who he needed and wanted, and he only required the strength to say it out loud. To own what he felt and take what he wanted, make her his, and the consequences be damned.

And be damned his father's rage that would accompany such an admission.

FIFTEEN

H ailey was admitted into the sitting room of Lila's home, her mother shutting the door behind them after tea, and a tray of biscuits was delivered for them to have.

Lila smiled, pouring the tea, and clearly pleased for a visitor. "I have not seen you in what seems too long. Tell me all your news. Are you looking forward to the ball? I must show you what I intend to wear before you leave for home."

Hailey took the cup of tea, sipping the strong brew just as she liked it. After her earlier exertions with Greyson, the tea was a well-needed repast. "There is much to discuss, and I'm glad I can have a catch-up with you. It has been too long."

"It has," Lila agreed, tipping her head toward the closed door. "Who is the young man who accompanied you? I have not seen him before."

At the mention of Greyson, her stomach fluttered. *He is everything wicked and wild and what I cannot have.* But she did not say that, not yet at least. "That is Mr. Everett. He works on the farm, normally in the stables, but sometimes in the fields. He's new."

"He's quite handsome for a stable hand." Lila giggled, a mischievous look on her face. "Is he agreeable?"

Hailey sighed. He was more than agreeable and had given her such pleasure, unlike anything she had ever known, that she already longed to experience it again. How would she keep from him? How would she behave? Hailey placed down her cup of tea. "If I tell you a secret, you must not say a word to anyone. not that I think that you would, but I need your promise in any case."

"Of course," Lila stated immediately. "You know that I'm as silent as the grave."

Hailey checked the door remained closed before she continued. "Against my better judgment, I have formed a sort of attachment with Mr. Everett. Both of us understand there is no future in our actions, but we cannot help ourselves. Whenever I'm around him, Lila, I'm overcome with a sensation I have never felt before." She paused. "I'm silently terrified that I shall never experience it again even when I find a man who wishes to marry me."

Lila bit her lip and reached for her hand. "While I'm happy that you have found a friendship with Mr. Everett, I can see your dilemma." She paused, silent a moment. "Would it be so very bad for you to marry a man of his station? I know we're both gentlemen's daughters, but other than our impressive dowries, we have little else to recommend us. Neither of us comes with property or connections. Marrying beneath us could not be so very bad, not if it were a love match. You could purchase a small estate, make a gentleman out of Mr. Everett and live comfortably ever after."

"I fear my parents will not agree with you. Mama

certainly would not." The thought of such a life material-
ized before her eyes, taunting her. Would it be so bad to
marry a man such as Greyson Everett? His passion, his
ability to give her what she wanted, looked promising after
today. Her bookwork ability and Greyson's farm skills
meant they could have a small estate and make it work.
And he was devilishly handsome. The way he looked at her
as if he wanted to gobble her up made her writhe. Something told her that to dismiss him would be a mistake she
would regret forever.

"But it is possible, Hailey. Let us be honest, neither of us
will ever make grand matches. In London next year, we will
not even circulate in that upper societal sphere. Your mama
must see sense, and maybe if Mr. Everett will wait for you
to return from town if you do not find a man whom you
would be happier with, your mama will see reason."

"I do dread going and being courted by men who do not
light an ounce of interest in me. What if we're made to
marry men whom we do not love or desire? Our lives would
be utterly disastrous."

"I shudder at the thought," Lila agreed. "That is why we
must be smart and listen to our hearts, not just our minds
or our family's wishes." She grinned, shifting closer. "Now
tell me, for I must live vicariously through you since no one
is courting me. What are Mr. Everett's kisses like? I know
he's handsome, tall, and muscular, but tell me what it's like
to be in his arms."

Hailey sighed, slumping back onto the settee. She knew
she had a whimsical look upon her face, but she could not
hide how she was beginning to feel. As if her life had finally
started, and there was a possibility, anticipation in her
future. She had been a reliable, intelligent, and loyal eldest
daughter of Mr. and Mrs. Woodville for so long. Now she

was possibly someone's love, someone's future. A woman who made a man's heart race.

"They are wickedly good, and when I'm in his arms, all I can think is I do not want to be anywhere else." And when she could kiss him again. They needed to spend more time together, but how to do that unless it was after his workday and she snuck out at night.

The idea had merit and sent somersaults to flip about in her belly. She would have to be so bold. There was no other choice if she wanted to be with him again, such as they were today.

"Oh, I do wish that I were in love and married. I long for my knight in shining armor to arrive, so I no longer have to live here in Grafton. Nothing exciting ever happens here."

"I know what you mean, but now that I've met Mr. Everett, I do not want to go to London at all. I will see how things progress over the next few weeks, and if my feelings grow and I know that I do not want anyone but Greyson, I shall speak to my parents. They will be disappointed and Mama possibly quite angry and upset, but when they see how happy I am with my choice, maybe there is a chance to change their minds."

But would Greyson wish to marry her? That she did not know, but today, he had not tried to take her fully when she was mindless with need. Had he tried, she knew that she would have allowed the intimacy and that in itself showed her he was not as rakish as he appeared.

The hunger she had read on his face, his hard appendage pressed into her thigh told her he wanted her as much as she had needed him, and yet he had not asked for more. She did not know if that was a ploy or because he was at heart a gentleman and would not cross that particular line. She hoped it was the case and that she was not wrong with his affection for her.

"I wish you all the very best, and know that no matter what your parents think, I shall be here for you, always."

"Thank you, Lila. I knew that I could count on you."

SIXTEEN

Hailey lay in her bed two days later and stared at the wooden beams above her that ran diagonally across the ceiling. The house lay quiet, save for the odd noise from a rattling window or creaking door. The servants long ago to bed. She looked over at her sister Isla and could hear the small snore that told her she was fast asleep, and it was time she went.

She pushed her blankets back, slipping from the bed and pulling on her pelisse over her unmentionables. She did not have time to dress fully, but her pelisse was thick and long and would hide anything she wore beneath.

Hailey shuffled on the slippers she had left by her door and was thankful her sister had left it slightly ajar when she came to bed. She stood at the threshold, listening for any voices or sounds, and could hear none.

Taking a determined breath, she stepped out into the corridor and tiptoed to the stairs before climbing down as fast as she could. She did not use the front door, preferring to exit the terrace off the parlor as it was the farthermost from her parents' bedroom upstairs.

The moonlit night gave her the ability to see, and she ran from the terrace and down the stairs, keeping to the lawns and toward the folly that overlooked the river. Her destination this night. A small bridge over a narrow part of the river came into view, and she could see a shadowy figure waiting for her there.

Her heart fluttered, and her stomach clenched when Greyson turned and smiled. His eyes took in her person, like a caress upon her skin, and she shivered. She would never tire of him looking at her. Nor would she ever tire of admiring his handsomeness.

"Good evening," she said, nerves making her unsure what to do now. Even though they had kissed and he had done other delicious things to her, she had not seen him much the past two days, and a rendezvous with a man was not a common occurrence for her.

"Good evening," he drawled, pulling her against him and taking her lips. The moment he kissed her, all Hailey's nerves dissipated. She clutched at his shirt, kissing him back, wanting him to know she wanted to be here, to be near him as much as he was her.

"Come," he said, pulling her toward the bridge and the small path that led up to the folly. "Let us be alone for a time."

She liked the idea of such a thing. Earlier today, while dropping off some paperwork for Mr. Oak to look over in the stables, she had slipped Greyson a note to meet her here. She had been worried he would not come, but he had, and she couldn't stop the grin that formed on her lips.

It did not take them long to make the folly and the moment they stepped into the circular structure she was pulled into Greyson's arms. His mouth took hers in a punishing kiss. His tongue tangling with hers, his hands running through her hair, holding her against him.

"I have done nothing but think of you these past two days. When I did not see you about, I thought that you may have changed your mind about me." The worry in his eyes made her heart stop, and she clasped his cheeks, needing him to know how untrue such a concern was.

"No, I did not want anyone to suspect anything since I asked you to accompany me to Grafton the other day. We were gone some time, and since I had never taken an escort in the past, I thought it may raise suspicion if I sought you out yet again.

A bench ran about the circular room, and Greyson pulled her to sit. "I tried to tell myself it was some reason such as that, but my mind kept coming up with other unhelpful thoughts."

She grinned, sliding next to him and slipping her arms about his neck. "You missed me," she teased, kissing him quickly. "Admit it."

His eyes twinkled with amusement. "Maybe I did. You have been quite the distraction since my arrival here. I look for you everywhere, and I hate to imagine you with anyone other than myself."

His words made her yearn for a life, a future with the man in her arms, how sweet and kind he was. How he had changed since he first arrived. A little too pompous for her liking, but now? Oh no, now he had settled in well and worked hard. And his kisses were utterly diverting.

"I'm not interested in a courtship with anyone else, Greyson. Just you." Hailey kissed him again, slower this time. His arms slid past her hips to her back, pulling her close. Her breasts pressed against his chest and made her blood pump fast. Her body wanted this. She wanted this.

She wanted him in any way that she could, even though her knowledge was limited.

"Not even Mr. Bagshaw. I heard that he is quite the catch about the county. I wonder why your parents have not pushed you toward him for a match instead of traveling to London."

"They have," she admitted, seeing no reason to keep that information from him. "Or at least Mama has. And at first, I thought that perhaps we would make a suitable pair, but...not anymore."

"Why?" he asked. "He is a gentleman, and you're a gentleman's daughter."

She studied him a moment, wondering at his inquiry. "Do you wish for me to make a match with Mr. Bagshaw? I'm certain that he would favor if I showed interest in his courtship," she asked, disappointment marring her good mood. She watched him, hoping that was not the case. She could stand anyone wanting her to marry Mr. Bagshaw, anyone, but Greyson. She did not want him wanting her to marry Martin, which meant that he did not want to marry her himself.

Being in his arms again, Hailey wasn't so sure that truth was something she could stomach.

G reyson shook his head, chastising himself for asking such a thing. But he knew why he had done so. Because Mr. Bagshaw, for all his uppity ideals, would suit Hailey better than he. They were from the same county, their properties were of similar size, and they had the same social sphere.

If she were to marry such a man, she would slip easily

into the role of wife and eventually mother in this county and become one of influence and status in Grafton.

If he were to marry her, she would have the *beau monde* watching her every move, just waiting for her country manners to make a fool of herself in some way and laugh at her until another caught their attention.

A future duchess or not, that would not save her from gossip and sly remarks at her grand match and elevation in society. Nor would his father be kind and welcoming to the family. He would dismiss her as he dismissed anyone who was not titled and rich. He did not want her to be the butt of cruel jokes and nasty comments.

He would hate to lead her into a ball and have anyone be mean to her, for he would then have to retaliate and bloody some noses. And he could not bloody a woman's nose, no matter what she said or did.

Yet, he did not push her away, tell her to return to the house and look elsewhere for a husband. He could no sooner hold back the flow of the Thames River than he could hold back what Hailey made him feel.

Alive for the first time in his life. Worthy and cherished by someone genuine. She was an elixir he could not stop wanting.

"I do not want you to marry Martin Bagshaw," he admitted, tipping up her face to his. He took her lips, losing himself for a moment in her. "I do not know how I shall bear seeing you go to London to find a husband. I know I should not want you for myself, but I do. I want us to stay here, locked away in the wilds of Northamptonshire where we never have to part."

She sighed, hugging him. Greyson started at the honest affection. He'd never been hugged before, and he liked the sensation of being in another's arms. A person who wished for no more from you than what she knew him to be.

Hailey did not know that he was a marquess and future duke. She did not know that he would inherit one of the most wealthy titles in England and one of the oldest. She knew nothing about him, yet she sat with him and risked her reputation to be alone with him.

A lowly farmhand with nothing to offer her but his love and affection.

She humbled him.

His heart tumbled, and he knew he was in trouble. His mind often warned him to take care, not tumble for any lady with a pretty face and handsome gown, but it was too late. He had fallen the moment she gave him his first set down, and there was no turning back from that.

Nor did he want to.

CHAPTER
SEVENTEEN

Hailey pulled back and stared at Greyson a moment, taking a deep breath as a multitude of emotions washed through her. Although she was not certain what any of them meant or would lead to, she knew she wanted to be with him. Give him affection and pleasure as he had afforded her.

"The other day, when we were alone, you touched me."

Greyson's eyes darkened, and he nodded. His Adam's apple bobbed up and down when he swallowed. "Teach me how to please you. I want you to have what bliss was afforded me."

"No," he shook his head, trying to pull away.

"Please, I know we cannot go any further than that, but there must be a way to satisfy you too. Let me try," she begged, sliding her hand down his chest, reveling in the feel of his muscles beneath her palm. Her fingers brushed the buttons on his breeches, and she slowly slipped them free of their bindings.

He covered her hands with his. "No, Hailey. I cannot ask that of you."

Hurt ran through her, and she paused her efforts. "You do not want me to touch you? You think I'm fast and unladylike, do you not?"

A deep, pained chuckle reverberated from him. "No, that is not the reason at all. I want you to touch me. I want more than your hand to touch me, but I do not want you to think that is all I want from you, for it is not. I would give you the world if I could. I would force you to wait for me so I could marry you and no one else."

Would he marry her? She touched him again, sliding her hand over the front of his falls, teasing the hardened appendage that pressed against her palm. "Why should we wait? If my parents agree to our union if they see that we have affection for one another, why would your father not do the same and agree we should be wed?"

He sighed, laying his head back against the folly's stone wall. "He's a miserable old man, determined to be cruel, not just to me but anyone. He also believes I should marry a woman of his choosing. I will not," he said, catching her eye and holding it. She could see he was determined and meant everything that he said. "I will marry who I want, but I fear it will not be until he is dead."

Hailey bit her lip, having never heard anyone speak of their parent with so much loathing and hate. But if one thing was certain, she believed Greyson hated his father. But why?

"And that is why you mentioned that I need to wait for you. Because you do not think he will like me and approve of our marriage?"

Greyson shook his head. "He would not. I'm sorry, Hailey. Even as a gentleman's daughter, he is set in his ways and thinks only of his own selfish needs."

"But that is just it, Greyson. I'm a gentleman's daughter

with a large dowry. Surely your father would not disapprove of me. That sort of thinking makes no sense at all."

Greyson cringed, rubbing a hand across his jaw. Hailey thought over his words, not understanding the dynamics of his family. One would think a marriage between a gentleman's daughter, an heiress, even if from the country, was a much better match for a laborer's son than he could ever hope. She did not want to appear snobbish or above Greyson in any way, but by birth, whether they liked the reality of that or not, it was true. He was beneath her in social status, and for his father not to want his son to marry up was not at all logical.

"I know it does not, Hailey." He sighed. "My father is a complicated man, and some say mayhap he should be in Bedlam. That is why I cannot marry you. Not yet, at least. Not until he is gone, and I know you will be safe from his ire."

"I do not care about his ire. I am wealthy enough to steal you away so we may make a life of our own somewhere else."

He chuckled, pulling her close and kissing her quickly. "That is if your parents do not take your dowry away from you for marrying a lowly farmhand."

Hailey swallowed, having not thought her parents would ever do such a thing. But then, her mama was determined to see her marry well. Would they deny her dowry to make her do as they wished?

"I do not want to talk anymore about families. They complicate things and spoil our time together," she said, changing the subject.

He chuckled. The deep, gravelly sound made her shiver. "Kiss me again and make us forget all that separates us, my beautiful, country lass."

Hailey needed no further enticement. She covered his lips with hers, taking his mouth with a need that bordered on desperation. He kissed her back, his tongue gliding and teasing hers. She moaned as his hand kneaded her breast, and no matter what he said, she needed to touch him. To give him what he so willingly bestowed upon her the other day.

Pleasure.

Release.

Satisfaction.

She slipped her hand beneath his breeches. The feel of his shaft, long and hard, was almost too much for Hailey to grasp. For a moment, she wondered how such a thing would fit within her, but then the pleasure that his hand afforded her told her that it would and that it would be delightful. Such release as she had found in his arms was in no way meant to be painful, and God knew what he was doing when he created man and woman.

"Show me what to do to please you, Greyson. Let me do this for you," she begged him, running her hand up and down his shaft.

He groaned, thrusting into her hold. "You are doing all that you should. Your touch feels wicked and good, Hailey."

A sense of fulfillment thrummed through her, and she could feel herself getting excited by his arousal. He kissed her hard, his hand twisted into her hair, holding her against him as his thrusts into her palm became more frantic.

Hailey held on to him, pulling at him with more vigor. He moaned her name, and she broke the kiss, wanting to watch him. To see what would happen to him when he found his release.

"Do you feel as I do when you touch me?"

He threw her a wicked grin, his eyes heavy with need. They burned with a fire that left her cunny wet.

"Oh yes, I feel as you did the other day. My release is as pleasurable. I assure you."

She tightened her hold, and he grasped the bench beneath them as if to keep himself from losing control. "Oh, dearest Hailey. You're killing me."

Wickedness took over her, and she leaned against him, kissing his neck. He shivered, and she grinned at his reaction to her. "Do you like it harder, Greyson?"

"Yes," he panted. "Make me spend," he begged.

She did as he asked, glancing down just as he moaned her name. Hailey watched, enthralled, as a creamy, white liquid spurted onto her hand and his shirt, his manhood pumping into her palm until he was spent.

She reluctantly let him go, helping him to settle himself back within his breeches before looking up and meeting his eye. "That was certainly unexpected. I had no idea that a man did such a thing."

He chuckled, pulling her against him. She lay her head on his chest, listening to the beat of his racing heart. "You undo me, Hailey. I fear I shall never want to let you go."

She kissed his chest, never wanting him to let her go either, and if she could convince her parents to let her marry him, to keep her dowry, they did not need his father's permission. They could live happily ever after without anyone causing any strife in their life.

"Me either," she admitted, content to listen to the river flow through her land as Greyson caught his breath. She could be with him like this, the two of them forever.

Her own happy marriage that she wanted to grasp with both hands.

CHAPTER
EIGHTEEN

The following day Hailey did not see Greyson about the stables or upon the fields where some of the workers now spent their days harvesting the ready crop.

Not that she was looking for him, she told herself. She was merely taking an interest in the farm and ensuring all was as it should be, just as she had for several years now. After all, she helped her father run the estate, and there was nothing odd about her being near the stables or walking the grounds.

She started toward the back of the house that led down to the river. Mayhap today Morris and Greyson had taken the horses for another dip, but when the river came into view, nothing but the fast-flowing water revealed itself.

Hailey sighed, not wanting to look like a cleaver toward Greyson, and instead took the opportunity to slip off her boots and stockings to dip her toes in the cool, refreshing water. The water was colder than she expected but pleasant. She leaned back on her hands, staring up at the sun and taking in the warmth.

She shouldn't, of course. No lady attended London with a face full of freckles, but she was no longer so worried about all that. Not if what she was starting to feel for Greyson was any indication. What did it matter if she left for London? If Greyson was starting to feel what she did for him, he would soon change his mind and ask for her hand. He would ignore his father's odd decree and perhaps even whisk her away to Gretna to say their vows.

She understood he did not want to cause trouble with his papa, but maybe if his father met her, he would like her enough to change his mind about Greyson marrying a total stranger. He may like her after all and condone the marriage.

She bit her lip, imagining their wedding night. His hands that were no longer so soft, slipping over her body. Bringing her to the peak of ecstasy he was so adept in giving her.

How would she ever get enough of his touch, of what they could do? Should they buy their own small estate and work it, she would never let him leave the marriage bed again. She would keep him there, hostage until she had sated her unexpected wants and needs.

"Miss Woodville, may I speak to you a moment?" a familiar voice that made her start said from behind.

Hailey sat up, heat running up her cheeks and neck. She stood, dusting off her dress. Her stomach twisted into a delicious knot at the sight of Greyson. His shirt was dirty and covered with dust and grime from whatever he had been working on.

He looked nothing like the man she ought to consider. Certainly, he was a laborer, not a gentleman, but her heart had other ideas, and she couldn't think of anyone else's arms she would prefer wrapped around her.

"Of course, what can I help you with?" she asked, feeling as though he did not want to discuss them, but something relating to the farm due to his serious expression.

He turned and checked that they were alone, and doubt lodged in her belly. Maybe the conversation would be about them. "Do you see that large willow tree hanging over the river just beyond your shoulder?"

Hailey turned and glanced behind herself, spying the tree he mentioned. As children, she and her sisters had pretended the tree was a magical fairyland where they would be whisked to unknown, mystical lands.

The thought of stepping under the willow tree with Greyson would be magical all in itself. "Yes, I see it," she replied, unable to keep the grin from her lips.

"Steal away with me there for a moment. I need you," he said, looking back toward the stables and pointing as if they were having a completely different conversation to the one they were.

She left her stockings and slippers on the river bank and started for the tree. It was an old willow, had been large even when she was a child. The long, hanging branches and foliage made them both disappear from view as soon as they were under it.

No sooner had she stepped out of sight were his hands wrapped about her waist. He pulled her against him, her back against his sweaty, hard chest, and she sighed at the pleasure it afforded her.

She shifted her head to the side, his lips grazing down the length of her neck, his small little nips along her vein making her shiver.

"I have missed you, and I've been looking for you. I saw

you head in this direction and knew that I had to come to talk to you."

She sighed, reaching back and slipping her fingers through his hair. "I'm glad that you did. I've missed you too."

"Will you tell Morris you had to speak to me should he chastise me for not working? I do not want to be a bad employee. My mistress may dismiss my lazy London arse."

She chuckled, shame washing through her that she had once thought him exactly that—a lad from London with no idea how to carry out farm work. "You have proven yourself to be capable of working quite efficiently, Mr. Everett. You have improved greatly since you first came here, and I will not dismiss you." She grinned. "And I will protect you from Morris's ire."

She could feel his smile against her shoulder. "You smell divine. Like rosemary." He kissed her jaw, and Hailey bit her lip, her body afire from his touch.

His hands skimmed over her stomach, reaching down to touch the apex between her thighs. She ached against his touch. She wanted him to make her reach the pinnacle that she had before. She could not wait the many hours until the house was quiet and the moon high in the sky before seeing him again.

She needed him here and now.

He pushed against her bottom, and she could feel the hardness in his trews. An ache thrummed between her legs, and Hailey knew at that moment that she wanted him. She wanted him to do more than touch her. She wanted him to be the first man she ever made love to—the first and last man to have her honor.

"You're so beautiful. So beautiful that you make my

breath catch," he whispered against her ear, squeezing her lobe with his lips.

Hailey turned in his arms and kissed him. Their kiss was wild, deep, and punishing. Her wits spiraled, and she clutched his shoulders, holding him as an anchor so she would not fall.

He reached down, lifting her gown to pool about her waist. For a moment, she wondered what he was doing before he lifted her off her feet. Hailey wrapped her legs about his waist as he took the few steps, her back coming up hard against the willow tree. He surged against her, and fire coursed through her blood.

"Greyson," she begged, his undulating making her moist and needy for him.

"I want you."

His words pulled her from the exquisite dream she was living. She met his eyes and knew what he said was true. She did not need him to tell her. His body gave him away, just as her own was.

"I want you too. I want you to be my first. No one else," she said, squirming against him. Her body shivered, and she ached in the most delicious way. Never had she felt like this. Even today, the feelings he evoked in her body were new and unknown—nothing like when he had touched her under the tree.

"I cannot. I promised myself that I would not ruin you."

She lay the palm of her hand over his cheek, feeling stubble against her skin. "I do not care about any of that. Please, I need you as much as you need me."

A pained expression crossed his features, and then she was standing again. Greyson kneeled before her, his hand hard against her stomach, making movement impossible.

He lifted her skirts, pushing the shift and gown out of the way. "I will not leave you unsatisfied, my darling," he said.

Hailey clutched at Greyson's hair as his mouth covered her mons, his tongue sinking between the folds of her sex and kissing, lathing her without remorse.

Her head spun with what he was doing. The odd sensation of his mouth in her most private and sensitive place. She bit her lip, clasping his head in her hands, and lifted her leg to sit over his shoulder. He groaned. The rumble of his reaction jolted pleasure to her core.

"Greyson," she begged, wanting more.

"I love your pleasure, Hailey. I could do this to you all day." His tongue did more wicked things. He suckled, and she almost buckled to the ground. "You're so sweet. I will never get my fill of you."

Her heart raced, and she closed her eyes, losing herself to the sensations he evoked. Again, she could feel the pinnacle, the long, delicious climb to ecstasy. And yet, this climb seemed faster, wilder, and unrestrained. She could not catch her breath, and she loved every moment of it.

He slid one then two fingers into her core, pumping into her, suckling and licking as if his life depended on her enjoyment.

Her body arched, and his hand's pressure against her stomach increased, and then she was flying, floating through the air as her body convulsed, spasmed against his wicked mouth.

Greyson lathed her until the very last tremor ran through her core. She sagged against the tree, thankful for its support.

He stood before her, a satisfied grin on his mouth before he took her in a kiss that stole her breath.

And her heart.
She was his.
From this day on.

CHAPTER
NINETEEN

Two weeks of utter bliss passed by for Hailey. Days of finding each other about the estate, riding horses to different locales about the county. Greyson accompanied her to visit her friend Lila again near Grafton, and they had even managed to sneak off for a picnic without being caught later that same afternoon.

The nights were what she lived for, however. Nights of talking under the stars, of being alone with Greyson was something she had started to long for. To be in his arms, kissed and pleasured in only the way he could satisfy her was like living a dream. She would remember the days as the best of her life, and she never wanted them to end.

Hailey stepped down from the family carriage at the Grafton Village ball. Tonight she wore a pink and cream silk gauze gown, the color and cut suiting her. Her mama had been kind enough to let her borrow her diamond earrings, and she felt quite the bell of the ball.

Hailey glanced across the road where other vehicles were dropping off attending guests and spied Greyson jumping down from a cart that sat several of their other estate workers.

His eyes met hers over the sea of heads. His gaze burned a path to her person. Her stomach fluttered in renewed need. Would she always have this reaction to Greyson? And if her parents should not allow her to marry him, or his father for that matter, would she ever be able to find this unexpected reaction with anyone else? Something told her to fight for Greyson, that he was who she wanted as a husband, no matter the differences that were issues at this time.

Lila called out her name, and she turned, finding her friend making a direct path in her direction.

"Good evening, Lila," she said, bussing her cheeks.

"I'm so glad you're here. Let us go inside," Lila said. "I'm so excited for the ball." They entered the hall, which was already a crush from the local gentry, townsfolk, and servants of nearby estates who were in attendance.

Hailey fought not to blush as several gentlemen, including Mr. Bagshaw, took in her appearance, their interest in her person clear to see. Tonight her maid had placed her hair into a motif of curls with white baby's breath placed throughout. Her dress shimmered in the candlelight, and she nodded, speaking to several people as they made their way into the ball.

Her parents placed themselves near the unlit hearth in the hall, a position they always took up, and it wasn't long before the orchestra started playing a lively tune and the dancing commenced.

Her sister Ashley was soon whisked onto the dance floor. And then a young man and laborer from a nearby farm asked Millie to dance. Hailey studied her mama and did not miss the tightening of her mouth in displeasure.

Hailey knew her mama would not say anything about it, not here and now, but her mother's reaction gave her pause. She did not like them to dance and interact with the servants, and tonight was the only day they were allowed to. If she were to ask for permission to marry Greyson, her mother's displeasure did not bode well for approval.

Tonight was for all the classes to enjoy the dancing, the music, and conversation, and drop the status and ranks that typically kept them apart.

She sighed. If only it could be like this always. If only people, no matter their wealth and class, could marry and love and be happy, no matter if they brought a great deal to the union or nothing at all, so long as love was foremost and strong within the marriage.

Hailey caught sight of Greyson standing several people away from her. She could hear his laugh and voice as he spoke with his friend Thompson and Mr. Oak, the estate's steward. Their conversation looked lively, and Greyson looked happy. His wide smile and bright eyes made her want to swoon at the handsome sight he made.

Maybe her ideals of different classes marrying were naive and nothing but a dream that would never be realized, but there was something about Greyson that she couldn't help but feel was right. He called to something deep within her soul, and she was unwilling to lose it.

"Mr. Everett is looking dashing this evening," Lila stated, sipping her ratafia. "But he does seem to be keeping his distance from you when it is not necessary. If anything, tonight is an opportunity to be with you without notice."

"I'm certain we will dance, but I think he is concerned that if we're seen together, it will spark talk." Their chemistry was unlike anything she had ever experienced before, and she knew she could not school her features when in his arms at just how much she loved being there.

Lila grinned, her eyes twinkling in mirth. "You do not need to be dancing to bring attention to your friendship. The fact that you both cannot stop looking at each other is more than enough to cause talk."

Hailey tore her gaze from Greyson to Lila and hoped that was not the case. Were people suspicious of them already? She needed to tell her parents long before gossip reached their ears if she had any chance of making her affections for Greyson known, and her wishes regarding their future. Should her mother hear Grafton's latest on-dit by anyone but herself, her plan to marry Greyson would be lost.

"I will be more careful," she promised Lila and herself, making an effort to look elsewhere about the room and smile at several gentlemen who were watching her and Lila.

"Miss Woodville, Miss York, how lovely you both look this evening," Mr. Bagshaw said to them both, bestowing a most elegant if a little too foppish bow before them. "I have been looking forward to this evening most adamantly, and I hope you have both come here ready to dance through the night."

"Of course," Lila stated. "But one must be asked to dance before one takes to the floor."

Martin ignored what Lila stated and held out his arm to Hailey. "Shall we dance, my dear?"

Hailey threw a knowing look toward Lila before nodding and taking to the floor. Numerous other couples joined them, lining up beside them as they prepared for a country dance. The overwhelming scent of sweat and the different fragrances in the room grew as more and more guests packed their way into the hall.

"I hoped that we may speak in private this evening, Miss Woodville," Martin said, standing across from her, his words drawing attention from those on either of their sides.

"If you wish," she replied, knowing there was little point in denying him. His character would not allow him not to get his way, and he would seek her out until he had said his piece.

Not that she wanted to hear, for she knew what he was going to say to her. That he wished her to be his wife and she would finally have to tell him that she, unfortunately, saw no future between them.

The music started and so too did the dancing. They moved in unison with everyone else, and even though she was dancing with a man she had no feelings for, she threw herself into the steps and made the best of the ball that only happened once a year.

The dance took them up and down the room, her breath labored, and her skin prickled with heat as it continued. The crush of guests increased and made the air stifling and uncomfortable. Other people seemed to be as affected as her. The ladies used their fans while the men imbibed the liquid substitute.

She glanced over Martin's shoulder and found Greyson watching them, his disapproving scowl and tight lips all she needed to see to know he was less than pleased she was in Martin's arms.

"You are so very beautiful this evening, Miss Woodville...Hailey, if you would allow me to be so bold."

She met Martin's eyes. They often used their first names, so she was unsure why he was acting as if this a new form of addressing each other. Did he want those about them to think that they had not addressed each other for years by their given names and that they were growing closer? That tonight may be the start of something more personal between them?

"Thank you, Mr. Bagshaw." She ignored his pout at not using his given name and instead concentrated on the dance.

She glanced yet again past Martin, and Greyson's scowl deepened before a young woman who worked as a maid at a nearby estate pulled him toward the dance floor to try to get him to dance with her.

Her stomach twisted at the sight of them blending in with the dancers—a lump formed in her throat when they came to stand beside her and Martin. During different parts of the dance, she was partnered with Greyson, and other than staring at her with a steely-blue gaze that gave little away, he did not say a word, although he seemed to speak well and freely enough with his dance partner.

Hailey shook herself from the melancholy that rioted within her. He was merely protecting her from prying eyes that may have noticed their interest in each other. He was not dancing with the young lady for any other reason than she was dancing with Mr. Bagshaw, merely doing their duty and making the night a pleasant one for all who attended.

Hailey moved through the steps without thought, knowing them as well as the back of her hand. The dance partnered her with Greyson once more, and he pulled her closer than was necessary. His hand slid up her arm, a little beneath the sleeve of her gown. Goosebumps rose on her skin as his finger circled over her flesh. His determined and heated gaze, all but alight with flames, flickered to life and made her ache.

No sooner was his touch upon her were they separated again, and she was back with Martin. No shivers, no longing or expectation thrummed through her in this man's arms, and she knew to the core of her very soul what she wanted, who she wanted.

The dance came to an end, and Martin escorted her back to her parents, chatting for several minutes with her father. Hailey stood near her mother, ignoring her mama's bright, knowing smile that darted between herself and Martin.

She would also have to tell her parents of her wishes that no matter if she was approved to marry Greyson or not, she could never marry Martin Bagshaw. The man irritated her. He was a snob and thought himself above everyone. A lifetime as his wife would be like accepting torture against oneself, and she would not do that. She wanted Greyson Everett, and even if she lost all that was promised to her, her dowry and reputation, all of it would be well lost so long as he was hers and she was his. Nothing else mattered.

CHAPTER
TWENTY

Greyson had imbibed on too much punch this evening. Not to mention he had watched with growing anxiety as Hailey was pulled onto the dance floor over and over again by a variety of gentlemen. Some local farmers whom he had met during his work at the Woodville Estate and others who owned businesses in Grafton or gentleman who owned modest estates.

All of them suitable matches for Hailey. Mr. Martin Bagshaw the front runner in his quest to earn her heart. This evening he was certainly engaged in trying to win her affection. But the man was blind. Did he not see Hailey's polite friendship meant nothing more than that? She did not look at him with longing, did not touch him as they spoke. If anything, she looked as if she wanted to bolt and run away from his exaggerated self-worth.

Thompson handed him another glass of punch, clearing his throat. "This one is spiked with brandy. There is only so much fruit punch a man can drink before one's teeth feel as if they are going to rot out of one's mouth."

Greyson nodded in agreement, sipping the punch that

now had a more flavorful kick.

"Miss Woodville is very popular this evening. I would think she will be off the marriage mart by the time the London Season comes around. And if not by then, certainly the first week in town."

Greyson ground his teeth, distaste filling his mouth at the thought. "She would not jump into any union she did not want with all her heart. I think your estimate is incorrect." Greyson had not divulged his growing feelings toward Hailey to his friend and valet. He did not want anyone knowing of their nightly rendezvous and bringing a stop to them. He found he lived for the evening, to be alone with her. Not just so he may take his fill of her sweet lips or give her pleasure, which they did often, but because he respected her opinion and enjoyed their lively conversations.

"Will you seek her out next year in town?" Thompson asked him, meeting his gaze.

Greyson frowned. "You are being very impertinent, Thompson."

"I am," he agreed, his eyes a little glassy with too much liquor. "But I've never seen you before so at ease with any woman, and she is utterly charming. Did you know that she gave young Billy a bonus, one pound for his birthday, yesterday? The young lad broke down in tears, and she had to console him. She has a heart of gold and would make a wonderful duchess one day."

"You overstep your bounds, Thompson," Greyson warned, even though Thompson's words resonated through him with nothing but warmth. She was kind and caring to her staff and would indeed make a wonderful duchess. He had little doubt that she could handle all the running of his numerous homes without breaking a sweat.

But his father was far from infirm. It would be years before Greyson was in control of his future, his own desires and needs. She would not wait, and he could not expect her to. He wanted to marry her, but how to do so when he knew his father would cut him off, throw him to the wolves until the day his sire died. Only then could he gain the fortune destined for him. But that could be years.

He ran a hand through his hair. He had brought on some of the difficulties himself by being here under false pretenses. The Woodvilles would think him a liar, a man who played with their daughter for his amusement. To act as a farmhand when one was a marquess was unforgivable. And if they did not allow Hailey to marry him and have access to her dowry, and his father did indeed cut him off for not marrying a woman of his class, they would only have Hailey's money to live on.

He frowned. He could not do that. She deserved better. He needed to convince his father that Hailey was his perfect match, no matter that she was only gentry and not noble. Surely with her dowry, she would be suitable. Surely his father wasn't such a bastard that he would cast him out and his wishes along with it.

"Just marry the chit and be done with it. If you're married in a church, your father can do nothing about it. Nor can he disinherit you, not really. He can make your life difficult and with a lot less coin, but that is all. One day you will be a duke no matter what your father says and does."

All true, and Greyson would be a liar if he stated he had not thought of such a thing himself.

But would Hailey say yes to an offer of marriage knowing his truth? He had lied to her. Repeatedly used their class difference as a cause for concern. Not that such a thing was not a difficulty, for it was. The *ton* would make it difficult for her to be accepted, future duchess or not. Not to mention his father. He did not want her to be shunned and excluded.

In all the conversations they had had, the many times she asked of his life, he should have told her. He should have confided in her that his father was a duke, not some tradesman who thought himself too high in the instep to allow his son to marry a country gentleman's daughter.

His father had wanted him to marry a woman of his choice, which was all true, but also a long way from the reality of it all. That the lady was, in fact, an earl's daughter, and he was a duke's son. He had lied so much, and she would not easily overcome his falsehoods.

If he wanted her to trust in their affection for each other, he needed to tell her who he was and soon.

"You know my father would make her life a veritable hell. Gentry born is not noble, and he would loathe her being part of the family. I could not submit her to such pain."

Thompson's attention settled on Hailey as she glided about the ballroom floor with a man Greyson had not seen before. He was tall and not unfortunate-looking, and Hailey seemed to be enjoying his conversation much more than any of her other partners this evening.

Something in his chest pinched, and he rubbed a hand over the spot.

"As long as you understand that if she does form another attachment and decides to marry, you will lose her forever. Are your father's distemper and threats worth such a risk? You must ask yourself if you're willing to live without her for the rest of your life and be content and happy while you do so. Or risk everything to have her at your side."

His hands fisted, and it took him some moments to calm the panic that ran through his gut at the thought of a lifetime without Hailey. As the dance ended, Mr. Martin came up to Hailey and her dance partner, placing Hailey's hand onto his arm as if they were already married. Anger thrummed through Greyson at the audacity of the man as they walked from the room.

Greyson handed Thompson his glass and without taking his eyes off Hailey, followed them. His strides ate up the distance between them as he followed them outdoors, and he knew at that moment that Thompson was correct. He could not live without her. He wanted her for himself, as his wife, and no matter what either of their parents threatened to do or, in fact, did to them, nothing would keep him from her side.

He turned about the corner of the hall and found Mr. Bagshaw on one knee, arms outstretched toward Miss Woodville, and the words *will you marry me* floating across the air to his ears.

Oh, hell no, you pompous flop. No one but me will be saying those words, was his last thought before interrupting them.

"I do beg my pardon," Mr. Everett said, halting not far from where Hailey stood and Mr. Bagshaw kneeled. Martin stood, his height nothing to Greyson's, and she fought not to laugh at Martin's attempt to look down at Greyson.

"I do not beg your pardon, Mr. Everett. Please leave."

Hailey did not miss the flexing of Greyson's jaw or that Martin seemed completely oblivious to the notion that he had possibly poked a lion intent on his prey.

"Mr. Everett, is there something that you need?" she

asked, stepping past Martin and hearing his huff of annoyance at her back.

"Your parents, Miss Woodville, they have asked me to fetch you."

"Utter lie," Martin spat, grabbing her arm with more force than was necessary. She tried to remove his grip, to no avail.

"Let go of Miss Woodville, Mr. Bagshaw." The low, steely voice brooked no argument. Again Martin seemed to miss the warning in Greyson's tone.

Martin pointed a finger at Greyson, almost taking out Hailey's eye in the process of getting his matter across. "You will bide your tongue, boy. I am the master here, and you are not. Now leave before I have you fired from your position at the Woodville Estate."

Greyson looked at Hailey, and she shook her head, willing him not to strike Martin. She did not want him to have any trouble, and certainly not with Martin Bagshaw, who was not worth the effort. What a snob the man was. How was it that she had never noticed before?

"Mr. Bagshaw, please do remember that Mr. Everett, no matter his position on my father's estate, deserves respect. If my parents seek my presence, I must go to them. You may call on me tomorrow if you wish to discuss the matter in which you were on your knee for then."

Greyson snorted, not helping Martin's ire. "You think this is amusing? How dare you, sir," Martin spat, surprising Hailey and pushing Greyson in the chest. That Greyson did not move and merely looked down on Martin as if he were some annoying yappy dog did not help the matter.

"Gentlemen, please," she said, coming between them, pushing them apart. "We will not quarrel." She let her hand drop from Martin's chest in an instant, but her other lingered on Greyson. The warmth and solid mass beneath her palm made her stomach clench in desire.

Martin stared at them both, narrowing his eyes. "Remember who you are, Miss Woodville. It would be a shame indeed if word got out about town that you allow your servants to talk back to their betters and I—"

"Enough," she said, cutting Martin off when he went to continue his bitter tirade. "We are not better than anyone else, and no matter who we are born as or what we do in life, no one deserves to be spoken to like they're nothing. Please go inside, Mr. Bagshaw, before you insult my farm-hand further and he is made to defend himself." She crossed her arms over her chest, glaring at a man she once thought kind and gentle.

Instead, Martin had a nasty streak within him and a littleness that had not shown its ugly self until recently. Not until Mr. Everett had commenced work on their farm.

"I know Mr. Everett is lying. I asked your parents before taking the air with you, Hailey, if I may ask for your hand in marriage. They would not recall you now."

She turned to Greyson, who merely shrugged, not an ounce of guilt crossing his features.

"Your farmhand has designs on you and seeks to ruin you. You must return to the ball with me."

"I shall speak to Mr. Everett first, Martin. Please leave me now. I shall be back inside soon enough."

Mr. Martin stomped off as if a child of three years instead of nine and thirty. "I shall return with your papa, and then we shall see," he muttered before he disappeared around the corner.

Hailey rounded on Greyson. "What on earth are you...oh."

TWENTY-ONE

Greyson didn't allow Hailey to finish her admonishment of him. Instead, he wrenched her against him and closed his mouth over hers, silencing any words she was going to say.

He felt a moment of denial, her hands pushing against his chest, but the moment he slipped his tongue into her intoxicating mouth, savoring the sweet wine that she tasted of, she melted against him. But it wasn't long before she regained her wits and forced him away with more power than he thought her capable of.

Greyson stepped back, staring down at her, her lips glistening in the moonlight from his kiss, her pretty green eyes heavy with desire. "What are you doing, Greyson? You cannot kiss me here in such a public location. Anyone could have come across us." She looked behind him, checking to see if her warning had come true. "Mr. Bagshaw may have followed through on his threat and fetched my father."

He ground his teeth, knowing full well what she said was true, even if he hated having to be away from her like a dirty little secret. "I followed you when I saw Bagshaw pull you from the hall. I could not allow him to be out here with you alone."

She scoffed, pacing before him, her long, pink skirts floating out behind her with each step. This evening, she was the epitome of beauty, a woman suitable for a king, not just a duke. Her hair, up and curled, accentuated her slender neck. Her very kissable neck that he craved to taste once more.

He reached for her again, and she slapped his arms away. "We cannot be caught together, not outside. We shall return to the ball and dance there. No one will suspect anything if that were to happen."

"I do not want to return to the ball," he stated, wanting only to be here with her.

"Really?" She looked surprised. "Are you not eager to return indoors? You seemed well-pleased dancing with several women who were not me."

He ran a hand through his hair, clasping it in annoyance. "Do be serious. At country balls, everyone dances and partakes in the fun. It does not signify anything. The only woman I want in my arms is you, as you well know."

She stopped her pacing, turning to face him. "I am being serious. You did not ask me to dance, and you had the opportunity."

"When?" he asked her, throwing up his hands. "You were not left alone. I could no sooner ask for your hand for a dance than to keep Martin Bagshaw from drooling at your slippered feet."

"Are you jealous of whom I danced with?" she asked him, raising one curious brow. "Do you feel challenged that a gentleman has done what you have not and asked me to marry him?"

Greyson cringed, hating that what she said was true. He

loathed the idea of anyone asking Hailey for her hand in marriage. She wasn't for any of them, she was his, and he was hers, and why they were even arguing this right now, he had no idea. He was jealous. He would admit that. Seeing her tonight in another man's arms made him seethe, and he wanted to chastise her for it while also pummelling the men who dared speak to his future wife, for he would marry her. He would marry her as soon as he was able.

"What gentleman offers marriage to a lady outside a country ball, might I ask? If you wanted to marry Mr. Bagshaw, I should not stand in your way. Is that what you want, Hailey?" he asked, calling her bluff. He crossed his arms over his chest, waiting for her to reply.

She narrowed her eyes. "What gentleman kisses and does all that we have been doing," she whispered, "and does not ask for her hand? No gentleman that I know acts in such an ungentlemanly way." She walked up to him, poking a finger in his chest. "Were you going to ask for my hand? Or did you merely want to ruck up my dress a few more times, have a little fun before you return south to London?"

He opened his mouth to reply, but no words spilled forth. Was that what she thought of him? A vagabond who used women such as herself and then left them to pick up the pieces of their lives when he wandered off once more? "I would never do such a thing. I was not raised to be so crass and without feelings. You know that I want you to be mine, but some things need settling first before that can occur."

She threw him a skeptical smile. "I do not believe you."

He clasped her hand, drawing her close. "I want you. No other woman compares to you. I think of only you. I was jealous, I will admit to that. I did not ask you to dance for I did not think I could hide what I felt for you if we did. I want to hold you close, run my fingers through your hair, kiss your sweet lips. I want all those things, and had I danced with you tonight, everyone, including your parents, would have known the same."

He ran a hand over his jaw, fighting to find the right words. "I cannot lose you, Hailey. I will not."

She stared up at him, her eyes bright with unshed tears. "I'm sorry," she said. "When you did not ask me to dance and to see you with that maid, I did not like it either. I suppose I was a little mad at you too."

"We were mad at each other, and you know why?" he asked her, wrenching her against him.

She shook her head, her hands splaying across his chest. "Why?" she asked.

"Because we're in love with each other, and you and I both know it." He kissed her then, lingering against her mouth a moment before pulling back. She followed him as if to keep the kiss from ending, and he bit back a knowing grin.

"Say you will not marry Mr. Bagshaw or anyone. Tell me that you will wait for me. That you will give me time, no matter what happens between us, that you will hold on to tonight and not let anything rip us apart."

A confused frown settled between her eyes. "What do you mean? Nothing could break what I feel for you."

Greyson hoped her words were true. "You know there are things in my life that prevent me from asking for your hand, from being with you as we both want. But know that in time I shall be able to marry you. That you are the only woman I want on my arm and at my side, the only woman to warm my bed and have my children."

A wistful look entered her eyes, and she sighed. "Do you mean all that you say?" she asked. "Why can we not throw ourselves at my parents' mercy and beg them to allow us to marry? If they grant the union, and I'm given my dowry, we do not need your father's approval."

Greyson wished they could do such a thing, but should she be outcast and his father cut him off financially, she would be left as destitute as he. He could not allow such a thing to become her life. Hailey deserved more than that. She deserved to be a duchess, to be his wife. And somehow, he would make that a reality.

"Believe me when I say that I'm going to fight for us, Hailey. That I love you and want you to marry me, but I must put things in place before we can take our vows just in case both our families do not agree to the union."

She watched him, fear and longing storming within her green eyes. "You speak as if you will leave me. As if you're saying goodbye."

"Not yet," he reassured her. But soon, he knew he would be summoned home. He had been here over a month, and his father's punishments never lasted much longer than that. Over the years, they had varied in severity, and this, by his parent's standard, was already longer than the previous ones.

He closed his mouth over hers, needing her with a hunger that surpassed all thought of where they were or who could come upon them.

Her mouth opened to him, her tongue tangling with his. His mind lost all ability to think, and the kiss turned into a raging inferno. A fire burned through his blood, her tongue, slick and soft, intertwined with his. She was passionate and free in his arms, giving him all that he wanted and more.

He held her captive in his arms, the fragrant night air only adding to the intoxicating sensations that rioted through his blood. Her mewling sighs. Her sweet gasps and hands that traveled into his hair and down his back, scoring the skin beneath his coat.

Greyson clasped her ass, lifting her against his raging cock, rolling her against his flesh. She cried out through the kiss, lifting her leg somewhat to push herself closer against his sex.

He wanted her to touch him, to stroke him. He walked them back up against the side of the hall, using the wall to pin her where he wanted her. A warning voice told him to stop, to halt this madness so open and visible to anyone who came about the side, but he could not.

Her mouth made him drunk with need, and her kisses, as wild and demanding as his, drove him beyond thought or reason. He wanted the woman in his arms by his side, not just now, but always.

And then he heard it. The booming voice of his father and ice ran down his spine, knowing their time, his freedom working her farm, of loving her, had come to an end.

TWENTY-TWO

Hailey looked up at Greyson and frowned. He had pulled back from the kiss and turned his head toward the front of the hall.

Reality slowly seeped into her conscience, and she listened and heard yelling and demands from a commanding, authoritative voice she could not place.

Who was that shouting?

"Come," he said, pulling her back toward the front of the hall. He let go of her hand just before they came to the corner. Greyson slowed his steps, his face schooling into one she had never seen before.

He looked guarded, cold and hard, and so unlike the man whom she had just been kissing around the side of the building.

What was going on?

They entered the hall, and she walked up to her parents, her mother's pale face sending dread down her spine. Others at the ball stared at the man and several other people who accompanied him. The music quieted until nothing but the hushed whispers over the curiosity of who their guests were, the only thing she could hear.

"Where is my son?" the man's booming voice commanded. The older gentleman's thinning gray hair made him appear as if he ought to be sweet, but something told Hailey he was not.

"I am here, Father," Greyson stated, stepping forward, and nodding. "What brings you to Grafton this evening? Are you looking to include yourself in the county's yearly ball?"

That was Greyson's father! No, it could not be. He worked for a duke, and this man, well, this man certainly was no servant. She glanced back and forth between the pair, not believing a word of it until she noted their similarities. Their strong jaws and mouths were the same, and they had the same aristocratic straight nose. But where the older man's eyes were ice-blue and cold, Greyson's had a warmth to his. A warmth that she had grown to love.

She started when the older gentleman scoffed. Hailey took in his appearance, and unease slid down her spine. His superfine coat was tailored to fit his form perfectly. The highly starched cravat tied about his neck didn't dare to wilt. The embroidered waistcoat and polished shoes gave the man an air of authority and prestige.

She frowned. What was happening here? Greyson was a farmhand, hired to work the fields and stables. Why would his father, be dressed in clothing much finer than her papa's?

She turned to her father, about to ask him what was going on when he stepped forward, her mother on his arm.

"Your Grace," he said, bowing. "As much as we are honored by your arrival, we must ask that you leave. You are not welcome here."

Hailey felt like throwing her arms up in the air at the absurdness of this all. Why was he calling the man Your Grace? And why did her mother look as if she had seen a ghost?

"Anne Woodville, or should I say, Lady Anne Murphy, the Earl of Smithfield's youngest daughter and, if memory serves me correctly, his biggest disappointment."

"How dare you, Derby," her mother seethed. "Leave, and never darken our county again. It is repulsed by your being here, and I will not stand for it."

Derby? The Duke of Derby? One of England's richest, most powerful peers and whose authority even Hailey had heard of here in Grafton? Was that man Greyson's disapproving father? And how did His Grace know her mama?

She looked to Greyson, but he steadfastly kept his eye on his father, not looking at her at all.

The duke laughed at her mother's words, holding his stomach as if what she said was far more amusing than it was. It was not comical at all. "I will not listen to a mere gentleman's wife," he spat the word, letting all of the people who remained in the hall to watch this interaction know what he thought of her parents.

"I'm here to collect my son, who from reports I have received, has been quite happily situated on your little farm. Is that not right, my boy?" the duke asked Greyson, looking to him for clarification.

Greyson clasped his hands behind his back and raised his chin. He looked like a man well used to being ordered about, like a soldier or something. Hailey wanted to go to him, take his hand and comfort him, but did not. This was all so confusing, and she wasn't exactly sure what was going on.

"Mr. Everett, is this true?" her father asked him. Hailey walked up to stand beside her parents, needing to hear him state that it was not. That all of this was a mistake and that the old, nasty duke was senile and in need of help.

Greyson looked at her father and nodded once. "It is true, Mr. Woodville. I am Greyson Everett, Marquess of Cadmael, and future Duke of Derby."

The people in the hall gasped, and mumbles of conversation started about. Hailey could hear everyone's shock while she could feel her own. Her heart thumped fast in her chest, heat kissing her cheeks.

Oh dear God, no. Greyson was not who he stated. He could not lie to her. Not about something so big as the truth of who he was. She met his eyes, and he looked away, shame clouding his gaze.

"Tell me that is not true, Greyson," she questioned, shaking off her mother's hand when she went to stop her.

"I am who I say I am, Miss Woodville," he said, watching his father.

The duke smirked, and Hailey had never seen anything so evil. "Miss Woodville, is it? Let me guess," he said, walking over to her. "The oldest child of Anne. You look like your mama when she was your age, before life working a country farm stole her beauty." The duke tipped up her chin, his hold of her jaw painful. She frowned, trying to tug from his clasp. "And your looks too will fade in time, and just as fast when you marry a country squire."

"Do not speak to her like that," Greyson said, his voice hard and cold.

"Come, we will return home," her mama said, taking her hand and pulling her from the hall. Hailey looked over her shoulder and saw her sisters running behind them, eager to be gone from the commotion. The duke stared after them, and Hailey knew their argument with the man was not over.

"We shall be along shortly," the duke yelled after them, striding toward the doors. "There is much to discuss."

The last Hailey saw of the ball was Greyson, standing in the middle of the ballroom floor, despair on his features. She understood the feeling well, for an awful sense of foreboding had settled on her shoulders and would not dissipate. She was not looking forward to their forthcoming discussion. Nothing good would come of it if anything, nothing but her ruination and her family's downfall.

TWENTY-THREE

They had brought two carriages to the ball, and while her sisters managed to escape into the second one, she was forced to ride with her parents. They stared at her, her mother's disapproving gaze making her feel as small and inept as an ant without legs.

"Tell me nothing has occurred between yourself and Lord Cadmael. That you have not ruined all your chances of a good marriage, Hailey."

Hailey thought she might break the bones in her fingers from clasping her hands so tightly in her lap. She swallowed and knew that she could not lie. The truth always came out in the end, and it would be best not to start telling falsehoods.

"I love Greyson. He's going to marry me, Mama."

Her mother laughed, a cruel and mocking sound she had never heard from her before. Dread settled in her stomach as if her mother knew something she did not. "Is he now? Are you sure, dearest? Are you certain that he did not just want to ruin you, play with you while he rusticated in the country? Pretending to be a farmhand when he was in fact here at his father's decree."

"You do not know that is the reason why he is here. You did not give them the time to explain," Hailey answered, her mind furiously working, thinking if this was indeed the case. Had he played her? Was she a little fool who had fallen into a rake's hands?

"And why do you think he was here? Do you think a marquess enjoys shoveling horse shit all day? Or cutting fields of crops under the summer sun?" Her mother shook her head, her father oddly quiet. "No, he does not. He was sent here as punishment and to cause strife, that I do know."

Hailey took a deep breath, needing to keep her panic at bay. There was a lot they did not know yet. She should not jump to conclusions. "And why is it that you're so certain? How is it that the duke knows you so well, Lady Anne?" she asked her mama, using the title afforded her mother, if indeed it was true she was an earl's youngest child.

"Do not speak to your mother with such insolence, Hailey. Apologize. Now," her father said, his eyes narrowed in temper.

"I apologize, Mama. Forgive me," she said, even though she needed to know, not just about her mama, but Greyson too.

Her mother swiped at her cheek, staring out the window. Her father clasped her other hand, squeezing it in support. "I do not know why the duke sent Mr. Everett here, but I can guess," her mother said, her voice sad. "He's loathed me for years, and I always worried that one day he would strike out. That he has hit out against my daughter was not something that I expected. I thought it was I who would suffer his ill humor."

"He is a prig and bully. We ought to send for the magistrate."

Her mama patted her father's hand, gifting him a small smile. "You know as well as I the magistrate will not help. Not against the Duke of Derby. No, we shall have to deal with him ourselves, listen to what he wants to say, and then send him on his way back to the hell in which he came from."

"Good plan," her father said. "I have birds to study tomorrow, and I do not need my solitude interrupted by some London arse."

Hailey smiled, but still, her stomach churned. "You are the Earl of Smithfield's daughter? Why have you never said so before, Mama?" she asked, needing to know.

"I was born a lady into a wealthy family, but I fell in love with your father, a country gentleman. My family was disappointed that I did not choose a titled gentleman. The duke wished to marry me, you see, and my father would have loved nothing more than to see me as a duchess. But I knew the duke was cruel and unkind. My closest friend, whom I had debuted with, married him instead. I prayed she would be happy, and I think it was only when her son was born that she was. Otherwise, I fear she endured more than my worst fears could ever realize."

Hailey frowned, unable to comprehend such horror.

"She passed away when her son was only a boy, and I was cast out of the family without a dowry. But I have never regretted my choice and would do the same again if I had to choose a second time. But the duke hated that I turned him down. He went after my father and robbed him of his fortune. My family lost everything not a year after my marriage to your father, and my father died only days after that."

Hailey could not believe what she was hearing. "But we have such large dowries, Mama. How is that?"

Her mother chuckled, looking at her husband. "Your papa was a country gentleman but far from impoverished. And while he may not have had the fortune that my family or the duke shared, he was not without funds. I tried to reason with my family, explain to them that while he did not have a title, that did not mean a thing, for he loved me and could financially care for me and any family we made. Not that I would not have married him had he been the poorest of estate owners, for I would have."

Her mother leaned against her father, dabbing at her cheeks. "The duke has sent his son, whether unbeknownst to Mr. Everett or not, to cause strife here. He has used you to strike at me and my choice all those years ago. He is petty and cruel and still holds hatred in his heart, even though it has been many years since I have seen him. He means to ruin you, Hailey."

"Well, he will not. I shall not allow him to. I love Greyson, and he loves me, and we will be married, no matter what the duke says."

"No, you will not," her father declared. "I forbid such a union. We want nothing to do with that family. To think we could share grandchildren with such a bastard makes my blood run cold. You will cease all communication with Mr. Everett or else."

"Or else what?" Hailey asked, crossing her arms over her chest. "How is this either Greyson's or my fault? Why should we pay for you and the duke's dislike of each other?"

"Because he has lied to you. You do not know that he was not involved in this scheme. We know nothing about what they planned. And now we do not know what kind of reception we shall have in London next year. What rumors and slurs the duke will spread about you."

Their carriage rolled to a halt, and her father jumped down. Hailey refused his aid and exited without assistance, striding toward the house. "Go to the library, Hailey. I can see several other carriage lamps coming up the drive. Our discussion with the duke is not over yet."

Hailey glanced up the drive, and sure enough, her sister's carriage along with three others rolled to a stop. She turned on her heel and went to the library as ordered.

She paced before the unlit hearth until her parents, the duke, and Greyson walked in and joined her. Hailey wanted Greyson to tell her that all of this was a nightmare, that nothing was true, that he had not spent weeks lying to her.

All the hours they were together, the many opportunities he had to tell her the truth, and he never did. Not once. Surely he could not be so cruel.

She watched him and could see he was putting a guard up, protecting himself for what was to come. She steeled her nerves and demanded herself not to cry, not in front of the duke, who seemed to enjoy other people's pain.

"Why do you not tell us what you want, Derby?" her father asked the duke as he came in and sat at her father's desk. Hailey could not believe the gall of the man. But then, as a duke, she supposed there wasn't anything that he thought he could not do.

"Well, to be honest, I sent my son here as punishment. You see, Miss Woodville," the duke said, catching her gaze, "my son did not respect the position he had in society. He gambled at the seediest locales, drank himself blind at our clubs, and not to mention whored himself about London without care. He even dared to gain himself a mistress and did all he could to make the dukedom the latest on-dit, the laughingstock of all London. But I would not have it."

Greyson looked at Hailey and his hands fisted at his sides. None of what the duke said was true, surely. And Greyson would disprove his words. He would. He would not let his father slander him so badly with falsehoods.

"What gentleman in town does not enjoy their lifestyle? We have had this argument before, Father, and like earlier, I'm afraid I still have to disagree with your view. I never brought shame onto the family, but I am ashamed of my actions here. The Woodvilles do not deserve to hear the rantings of an old man, long past his prime, his only motive to be mean and cruel to his family and anyone whom he can strike out at."

"Silence," the duke commanded. "Even here, you continue to whore yourself. You have not learned your lesson, have you, son? You are sticking your wick in the Woodville chit's cunny, sneaking about the estate day and night without regard to her reputation or your own should her father demand that you marry her when you are caught."

Hailey looked to her parents and saw the horror, the disappointment in their eyes. "I have not lain with your son, Your Grace. You are mistaken."

The duke scoffed, and her mother came over to her, taking her hands. "My daughter would never touch anyone whom you sired, Derby. I am as thankful today as I was twenty-five years ago that I did not say yes to your offer of marriage. You and your son are no longer welcome here, and I ask that you leave."

Hailey turned to Greyson. "Do you have a reputation in town? Do you have a mistress?" She had to know before he left. The idea that she would not see him again broke her heart in two, but the idea that his father was right about his character shattered it into a million pieces.

He had said so many sweet, loving words to her. Were they all untrue? Had he merely said them to try to get her to lay with him? Certainly, there had been many times that they almost had, but he never did.

"Hailey," Greyson said, stepping toward her but stopping when her father stepped between them. "What my father says is true. I have a reputation and a mistress, but that is all over now. After meeting you, I promise you I would never return to such idleness knowing that I had you to return to."

"You will never marry my daughter. We want nothing to do with the Derby dukedom," her father spat.

The duke laughed, slapping the desk before he stood. "That is very good then, for I would never allow my son to marry some country booby's daughter who will never be accepted into my family. We are one of England's oldest and proudest lines, and I would never sully it with a woman who whored herself to a common farmhand. What other men has she lain with? How many servants does she allow to lift her skirts? She is as much a whore as your wife, Woodville. How proud you must be."

Hailey stood, stupefied, unable to believe what he was saying. Her mother stormed to the duke and slapped him. Hard. The crack in the room was all they could hear for a moment before the duke laughed, the sound maniacal. "I will admit, I always enjoyed your fire, Anne." He stormed from the room but stopped just as he reached the foyer. "We look forward to seeing you in London next year, Miss Woodville. And do not forget to send felicitations to Greyson, for he is betrothed. The announcement goes in *The Times* tomorrow."

"What?" Greyson asked, following his father.

Hailey slunk down onto the settee, not wanting to hear another word, not from anyone. But she could hear Greyson arguing with his father.

"To Lady Francesca, the Earl of Lincoln's daughter. Do not play coy, my boy. You knew of her and agreed to marry her. Her father consented, and you will return to town and marry. It is your duty, after all."

"I will not marry her. I do not love her."

"Look at them," the duke said, turning Greyson toward Hailey and her family. She glanced up from the settee, meeting his eye. "They are pathetic. Social climbing joskins not worth our time. The notice will be in *The Times* tomorrow, and the betrothal will be arranged. Your future is bright, while the Woodvilles, just as the Earl of Smithfield, will come to realize that you do not play the Duke of Derby a fool without being burned. No matter how many years it may take for justice to be served." He chuckled. "The sight of them, crushed and upset, makes up for all the years I had to wait for this day."

The duke slapped Greyson on the back before starting for the door. "I expect to see you in London tomorrow. My steward, Gerald, is making arrangements for you now. He will accompany you and Thompson to town." The duke turned to Greyson and pointed at him. "Do not think to stay, or do anything foolish, for I have eyes on you, and you will not get far."

And then he was gone, and Greyson stood alone in the foyer. "Mama, Papa, I need a minute with Greyson. Alone, if you please."

"I do not think..."

"Come, Anne. Let Hailey have her say to the boy," her

father said, walking her mother from the room and toward the stairs.

Greyson glanced over his shoulder, meeting her gaze before turning and walking into the library and shutting the door.

TWENTY-FOUR

Hailey crossed her arms, feeling as though she needed to protect herself from what he was about to say. What she had a horrible feeling was the truth.

"Do you have a mistress? Is that true?" she asked him, swallowing the lump in her throat that would not dissipate.

He sighed, running a hand over his face. "I had a mistress when I left London. I no longer have a mistress."

So he was like so many other men in town, but if he said that he no longer had a lover, she had to believe that was true. He certainly seemed as if he were telling the truth. And yet, that he had lied to her for so long, she wasn't sure what was false and true anymore anyway. "Why did you not tell me who you were? Who you really were?"

He walked over to the window, and she looked past him, seeing the ducal carriage pull away from her home. "I was sent here as punishment, to do manual labor because of my wayward lifestyle, as my father states. But I did not come here to fall in love. I did not think I'd meet anyone like you, Hailey," he said, turning to face her. "I should have told you the truth. I should have trusted that it would not make a difference to you."

"You're right, you should have trusted me, but you did not." She shook her head, her stomach full of knots. She felt as though she would be sick. "Did you not tell me because you believe as your father does? That we're nothing but cunning baggage?"

He came over to her, taking her hands. "No, of course not. But..."

"What do you mean, but. You do," she accused, stepping back. "It is not my fault your father is cruel and unkind and sought to strike out at my mother. But, nothing, Greyson. You did not trust me, not enough to tell me what your father had done and why you were here."

She thought back to all the things they had done together, the pleasure, the teasing and hours of discussions. Even after all the time spent together, she did not know who he was. She did not know him at all, only a version of him that was not who she thought he was.

"I was going to say that I am concerned about our social positions. Not for myself, but what the *ton* will think of you. How they will treat you. They are not the most accepting or kind group of people, and I fear they will make you pay for daring to marry a future duke. Marrying up, as some would say."

She scoffed, unable to believe he said such a thing. "You believe I would be marrying up. My mother was an earl's daughter, that tidbit is true, and my dowry is larger than I think you understand, not that it will factor in your life, for whatever it was that was between us is over. I could not marry into a family who thinks I'm a jade deserving reproach. You cannot possibly love me, or you would have told me the truth and not allowed me and my family to be ambushed by your father. Insulted without a by-your-leave from you."

A muscle worked in his jaw, and he stared at her. "I never meant to hurt you, Hailey. Never," he said.

She bit the inside of her lip to stop her tears. "The hatred between our families is more than enough to keep us from ever agreeing to an understanding. We will forget all that has passed here these past weeks and never contact each other again. I shall not seek you out or speak unkindly of your family, and if you can promise me your father will not slander our name in London, that will remain the case."

She could not have a Season, attempt to fix the fatal error she had made with Greyson if her name was no better than mud. "I doubt our paths will cross again in town. Our social circles being as different as they are. Can you promise me that if you cannot promise me anything else?"

"Hailey, please," he said, attempting to take her hand.

She slapped him away, not wanting him to touch her. If he handled her now, she would break, she was sure of it, and would never sew herself back together. When she made her room, then she could cry, hide and heal during the next few months, but not now. Not in this room.

"Promise me my reputation will be intact when I arrive in town."

He ran a hand through his hair, leaving it on end. "It will be as if you had never seen my father or me. I promise you." He started for the door, and Hailey could not help but follow his progress. She took in his pained features to memory, needing to keep them locked in her mind forever.

"I wish you well with Lady Francesca, my lord," she said, unable to hide the scorn from her tone.

Greyson turned, staring at her. His eyes were as glassy as hers. *Not yet, Hailey. Do not cry yet.*

"Goodbye, Hailey," he said, opening the library door and striding across the hall.

Hailey did not move, merely watched as another carriage rolled past the window a moment later and down the drive. She sucked in a breath, not having known she was holding it, and slumped onto the settee. Pain tore through her body, aching, severing pain, and then and only then did the tears slip down her cheeks. He was gone. The man she loved and had pinned so many hopes and dreams upon was destined to be nothing but a memory.

A nightmare she could not escape.

Greyson stormed into his father's library and slammed the door on the butler, who tried to stop him from interrupting the duke. "How dare you do what you did to Hailey and her family. How dare you treat them as if they are not worth the dirt beneath your boots."

His father smirked and leaned back in his chair, lifting his boots up on his desk, a small amount of grime falling onto the mahogany top. "Why should I not dare? They are worth no more than the dirt beneath my boots. Anne Woodville deserved the set down she received. It was a long time coming."

Greyson held up his hand, halting his father's words. "Because she would not marry you." He came over to the duke, leaning on the desk. "A quarter of a century later, and you are still angry over her choice." He shook his head, unable to fathom such behavior and certainly unable to forgive such unkindness. "How could you use your only son to get back at a woman who no longer featured in your life?

That you hurt her innocent daughter merely to get some kind of wicked vendetta that you seemed hell-bent on having."

"Innocent?" his father scoffed. "Do not forget I had eyes on you, Greyson. She was not better than the dock whores who warmed your bed. She spread her legs whenever she had a chance, and you damn well know it."

A wave of anger, so deep and loud, roared up through him, and Greyson lifted the duke's desk, tipping it on its side. Parchment, ledgers, ink, and quills spilled to the floor, and the force of the overturned desk shoved the duke back against the wall on his chair.

Greyson stormed over to him, leaning over the bastard who had caused so much pain, so much hurt. Not just to the Woodvilles and Hailey but to himself and his mother. She would die all over again if she knew how wicked her husband had become.

"I will marry Hailey, I will fight to gain her love back, and when I do, I will love her and ask every day for her to forgive the sins of my father and myself, and there is nothing that you can do about it."

His father's eyes went mad with rage, and he stood, but Greyson did not move. He was younger, stronger, and a good half a foot taller. The duke no longer scared him, and that was all he was to him now, nothing but a title. Not a father, never a loving parent. The only loving parent he ever knew was long buried.

"You will not disgrace our family or your betrothed by running off with that Woodville chit. She is a commoner, ruined trollop, and I will ensure her name is sullied should you go against me on this."

"I will not do as you say. I do not care what you do

about London. I will marry her and damn you all to hell." Greyson started for the door.

"I will ruin her name and do what I did to her grandfather, the Earl of Smithfield. I will ruin the Woodville family, ensure none of those five girls receive their dowry, all of them ruined and without hope of finding a match. Is that what you would do to them all? Your love is not so very great if you would make them suffer."

Greyson closed his eyes, wishing his father would expire. Leave this life so he would be free of his cruelty. "I will one day be the duke, and I will gain my fortune. You may win today, but it will not always be the case, old man. One day all of this will be mine, and even if I have to wait years to do so, I will marry Hailey, and not even your madness can reach beyond the grave."

His father chuckled, calling out to the butler to clean up his son's mess, but not before he yelled several last words. "Do not be so sure, Greyson. Death will not impede me. It is merely another tool."

Greyson left the ducal estate, never wanting to return. The man was mad, and he could live in his grand house with his abundance of money. He wanted no part of it. No part of him ever again.

TWENTY-FIVE

G reyson woke late in his bachelor house on Hanover Square, the sound of his housekeeper's incessant knocking on his bedroom door pulling him from his dream of Hailey.

He sighed, rolling onto his back, laying his arm across his eyes as the light streaming in through his windows insulted him. He groaned. Maybe he had imbibed too much wine last night.

"Lord Cadmael, may I come in?" More knocking. "My lord, it is urgent."

He called her to enter and sat up in the bed, blinking to clear his vision. "Mrs. White, what is it that cannot wait?" he asked her before frowning at the pale countenance of his normally jovial servant.

He threw back his covers, glad he had slept with his breeches on last evening and went to her. "Mrs. White?" he asked again when her eyes filled with tears. "What is wrong?" Had something happened to Hailey? He would never forgive himself if that were the case.

"Lord Cadmael, it is your father, the duke. He is dead."

"What?" Greyson stumbled back. Sure he had mistaken what he had heard. *Dead?* His father was more than alive and his usual, vicious self last evening. How could he be dead?

"I do not understand."

His housekeeper wrung her hands, pointing to the door. "There are men downstairs, my lord. Your father's steward is one of them. They want to speak to you."

Greyson grabbed a shirt that lay over a nearby chair and raced from the room. It did not take him long to go downstairs, and he entered his library to find his father's steward Gerald and Mr. Olivers, who was his father's solicitor.

"Your Grace," Gerald said, bowing. Mr. Olivers did the same, and regret settled in the pit of Greyson's stomach. Was it true? Was his father dead?

"We regret to inform you that your father, the Duke of Derby, suffered a seizure of the mind sometime through the night. He regained consciousness for a time this morning but then seemed to suffer another and has unfortunately passed. We are sorry for your loss."

Greyson started at Gerald, knowing full well what sort of man he was. His father's underling and evil aide. "And you did not think to send for me after his first seizure?" he asked, pinning Gerald on the spot.

"The duke requested that you were not to be informed."

The smirk from the man was beyond Greyson's tolerance, and he smiled back at him. "Gerald, your services are no longer required. Henceforth, you are removed from your duties as the Duke of Derby's steward of all my estates. Go back to the ducal town house, pack your things, and do not let me see you shadow my door again."

The man's smugness fell from his features, and Greyson pushed down any remorse that he was being too harsh, that Gerald too was merely a puppet for his father to play with. He knew the bastard had known what his father was up to sending him to Northamptonshire. He always knew what the duke was doing, his devious plans, and cruelty. Gerald was as bad as his father and deserved no sympathy from him.

"But I have worked for the duke for years." The man raised his chin, disdain shining from his cold eyes. "You will need to write me a recommendation so I may find employment elsewhere."

Greyson scoffed and shook his head. "You are dismissed. Go before my boot kicks you from this house."

Gerald took heed of his warning and left without another word. Mr. Olivers turned back to Greyson. "I have my carriage here, Your Grace. You are needed back at the ducal town house. There is much to discuss after what has occurred."

Greyson nodded, forgetting about the steward, and instead turned his attention to what was to happen. "I will dress and be out soon. Please wait for me. I shall not be long."

"Of course, Your Grace."

He flinched at the use of his title. No longer Lord Cadmael, but now the Duke of Derby. It was almost impossible to believe that his father was indeed dead. He had always thought the man would live forever. Certainly, his devil work on earth he always believed kept him safe from parting from this mortal life. If the devil had an ally here, why call him home, but alas, it seemed that was not the case. His father was dead, and finally, he was free of him.

Greyson had paid his respects to his father, whom the staff had laid out in his suite of rooms upstairs before he ordered the undertaker to take him away until the funeral, which he would hold at his country estate in Kent.

The family mausoleum was there, and as much as it pained him to lay his father to rest beside his dearest mother, that was where the duke would be buried. Just like all the Derbys in the past and future would be.

His father's solicitor slid several documents toward him, and he glanced down at them.

"This is your father's final will and testament. You are, of course, named as heir, as per your birthright. The ancestral estate in Kent, the Scottish hunting castle, and manor house in Ireland are entailed to you too." Mr. Olivers cleared his throat, placing his hands on the table, a light sheen of sweat over his lip. "There is one thing that I must disclose, Your Grace, and I beg your forgiveness for my inability to complete what the late duke requested of me."

Greyson looked up from the large figure of his worth and met Mr. Olivers' eyes. "What is it?" he asked him.

"As to that, one of your father's last requests of me was to draw up a marriage contract between yourself and Lady Francesca Lincoln."

Greyson swore. Damn it all to hell. He had forgotten that notice was to be printed today in *The Times*. He glanced at the clock on the mantel and knew it would be too late to stop the notice from going to press.

He ran a hand through his hair. With it printed on one of the most-read newspapers in London, he would never be able to get out of such an understanding even if he did not authorize the understanding. The *ton* would never believe it, nor could he as a gentleman break the engagement unless Lady Francesca wished to do so.

He cringed. From memory, the woman who unfortunately resembled his horse would jump at marriage to a duke since few offers were coming from anyone else. No matter how wealthy she was.

"You do realize that I never offered to Lady Francesca and do not wish to marry her."

The solicitor's eyes widened, and Greyson frowned. Was that relief crossing the older gentleman's visage?

"I forgot, you see. My daughter's birthday was yesterday, and I was already running late when I remembered that I was supposed to send the announcement to the paper for inclusion in the next print run. Your father did, in fact, charge me with placing the notice in the paper before he traveled to Northamptonshire, but the notice itself was not to be included until today. Forgive me, Your Grace. I will have the notice in the paper by tomorrow at my expense."

"No, you will not," Greyson said, relief pouring through him and making his head spin. London did not know of his father's devious plans. No one knew, and therefore, he did not have to marry Lady Francesca. He could marry whomever he wanted, and there was only one lady he knew he wanted at his side.

Hailey.

"I will not, Your Grace?"

"No," he repeated. "My father was forcing that marriage on me, Mr. Olivers. I will not be marrying Lady Francesca, for I neither know nor love her. But what you can do is draw up a marriage contract between myself and Miss Hailey Woodville of Northamptonshire. After I have settled my father's affairs and hired a new steward, buried my father at the Kent estate, I shall travel back to Grafton and offer marriage to Miss Woodville."

The solicitor stared at him a moment before he seemed to gather his wits and start taking notes. "Is Miss Woodville expecting an offer of marriage?"

"No," he said, seeing no reason not to state the truth. "And I daresay she will take some convincing to trust me again, but I will win her confidence and her love, and she will be the next Duchess of Derby."

Mr. Olivers smiled, clearly relieved, and started to fold his papers back in a leather case he carried with him. "I foresee no issues with regard to your father's will. I would like to take this opportunity to offer both my condolences and congratulations on succeeding the dukedom, Your Grace. I wish you well with it all, and please, do not hesitate to contact me should there be anything that you require assistance with."

Greyson stood, bringing the meeting to a close. He shook the man's hands. "Thank you. I will be, of course, keeping you on as my solicitor. I will be in touch if and when I need anything further."

"Excellent, Your Grace. Good day to you."

Greyson watched him leave and sat, staring out over his father's library, where only last evening he had overturned the very desk he sat behind. There were no reminders of his lapse in control. The room looked the same as usual, but the heaviness, despair, and dread the room always hovered within was gone, and with his father's demise, so too the fog of suffering the house carried with it.

He shivered, glad that he was gone. A terrible, ungrateful emotion to feel, but his father had never shown him any love or respect. He was the worst of men, and Greyson had little doubt when he laid him to rest in Kent, it would be only him at his graveside.

A sad legacy he promised himself he would not repeat.

CHAPTER
TWENTY-SIX

ailey sat at the dinner table and pushed the slice of cottage pie around on her plate. A month past, they had received word that Mr. Everett, really Lord Cadmael, had lost his father to a seizure of some kind not long after his return to London.

The paper had stated the new duke had traveled to Kent to lay his father to rest, but nothing else.

Feeling many eyes on her, she glanced up and found her mama watching her. The usual fear and pity she always looked at her with these days clear to read.

"Mama, do stop looking at me as if I'm going to smash into a million pieces. I'm perfectly fine." Perfectly fine was also another thing she had come to repeat daily. Her sisters shadowed her about the estate, talking of busy nothings and keeping her company.

She enjoyed having them at her side, but no matter how much they tried, it did not change what her heart felt with each pump in her chest. The day Greyson had left had near broken her in two, but to know that he was now the Duke of Derby, a man who could wield his future without his tyrannical, overbearing father ordering him about and he had not come to her, proved his words, the false promises, were worthless.

He had used her and was not coming back.

"If you have finished your dinner, my dears, you may be excused," her mother said.

Hailey went to stand. "Not you, dearest. We would like to speak to you a moment."

She sat back down, ready for yet another lecture on how to be happy and not sad at what Greyson had done to her. How he had treated her. How he had allowed his father to insult her family without saying barely a word to stop him.

She had heard it all before. Many times over the past four weeks and her patience in listening to the hollow words was coming to an end. She could not take much more. Some days, she felt as though she wanted to scream at the universe, curse, and throw stones into the air at how unfair life was, especially for a woman.

But what did the duke call her? No better than a trollop. Social climbing joskins.

"There is news, my dear, and we thought it better that you hear it from us instead of reading it any gossip rag or through those who like to talk of others' lives in Grafton."

Hailey downed the last of her wine, feeling as though she was going to need the fortitude of her drink for what was to come. "What is it now that I must endure?"

"There are two things," her father said, the pity in his eyes almost too much to stand. "Mr. Martin Bagshaw is engaged to a lady from Crofton. It is said that he met her at the Grafton ball not long after we departed."

Hailey scoffed. The man seemed to be as unfounded as Greyson for all his fancy words and declarations of wanting her for his wife. Were all men as fickle? Did they all think women were willing participants in their games to gain a wife?

Well, she would no longer play such contests. After her atrociously bad judgment, she was done with the male species. She would become a spinster, living with her parents until they passed and then becoming a burden to her sisters.

A perfectly acceptable plan.

"Well, at least I'm safe from that oaf," she said, ignoring her mother's gasp.

"Hailey, Mr. Bagshaw has been nothing but kind to you and I—"

"He believes himself above everyone, Mama," she said, cutting off her words. "I believe that if I had continued to think him worthy of my hand, I would have eventually poisoned his dinner within a few years of our marriage. I do not care what Mr. Bagshaw does or whom he marries. He speaks down to people, and I do not like it."

"Well, I daresay," her father mumbled. "Are you angry, my dear? You seem a little put out."

Hailey took a calming breath. She was angry, but her parents did not deserve her ire. Greyson did, however, but he was not here. He was in Kent at his estate, pretending to be a gentleman, no doubt. He was right at this minute, probably courting a bevy of guests at his estate who wished to enjoy the little season out of London.

Her mama cleared her throat. "The other piece of news is something your father and I have kept from you for a day or so, but we know that we cannot keep it from you any longer. There will be talk in the county, and we wanted you to hear the news from us before anyone else. This news we fear will upset you greatly."

Dread settled in her stomach like a musket ball, and she

steeled herself for what she was about to hear. "Go on," she said, folding her hands in her lap, lest she pick up the knife and throw it at the wall and cause injury to anyone innocent.

"The Duke of Derby has been written about in the paper two days past. He has been seen in Hyde Park with Lady Francesca. It was said that they seemed happy and comfortable in each other's company, and there is talk of a betrothal any day."

"I thought his father had already announced their engagement."

"It did not go into the paper as threatened. I checked when we received *The Times* later that week."

Hailey shifted on her chair, the lump in her throat, the constant companion that rose its ugly head each time she thought of Greyson, returned with a vengeance. She picked up her water, sipping it and hoping it would not choke her.

"Well then, that proves it, does it not? Greyson was a bastard who lied to me." She swiped at her cheek, angry that she was crying again for a worthless London fop who did not deserve her tears.

"It does seem to be the case, my love," her father said, taking her hand and squeezing it a little, understanding instead of chastising her for her language. "But it does not seem the duke was able to sully your name in town, and a Season in London is still possible if you wish to go, that is. We will not force you. The choice is yours."

"I do not want a Season. I want nothing to do with the London social scene. I just want to remain here."

"I refuse to let you wallow in your sadness and allow the previous Duke of Derby to win. He did not win against me all those years ago, and I shall not let him beat my daughter. You will go to London, and you will be the diamond of the Season, and you will show the current Duke of Derby that his choice to marry Lady Francesca was a mistake, and his choice should have been you."

Hailey's lips twisted into a small smile at her mother's words. "Maybe in the new year I shall feel differently about having a Season, Mama, but right now, I do not want to consider it at all."

"The duke is a fool if he marries Lady Francesca simply because his father ordered him to. I did not sense that he wanted any part of such a union, but mayhap I was wrong in my judgment of him that night they were here. It was, after all, a very heated discussion. I doubt any of us were thinking clearly or seeing people as well as we have in the past. Our judgment was skewed by the events of the night," her father said.

"I know that we said that we did not wish for you to marry Lord Cadmael due to who his father was and our association with that family all those years ago, but your father and I have discussed the matter, and we no longer feel that is fair. It is unfortunate that the man who seems to have captured your heart is the late Duke of Derby's son, but that is neither his nor your fault. I knew the duke to be a mean, vindictive man, and I think before any of your life choices are made, you need to listen to Lord Cadmael's side of the story. I do not think he was aware of the history between our families, and I think he too was used as a pawn for his father in a game he did not know he was playing."

"He's the Duke of Derby now, Mama, no longer Lord Cadmael or Greyson Everett as he led us all to believe. If he were not a willing participant, why is he not here, begging my forgiveness?"

Her mama sighed, nodding. "I should have seen the similarities earlier," her mother chastised herself.

Hailey frowned. "What do you mean?" she asked.

"Well, Everett is the family name of the Duke of Derby. So Mr. Everett was, in fact, Greyson Everett, Lord Cadmael before ascending the title of duke."

So not all a lie, but still, he had not told Hailey the truth. "It does not change that he chose to keep his identity from me. As if I were some poor country mouse who did not deserve him or the truth of who he was. Even when we became close friends, I cannot help but think he thought me a social-climbing whore."

Her father met her eyes, his steely gaze making her pause. "How close, Hailey? Is there a chance that you are hiding anything from us, for we need to know now before more weeks pass."

"I did not give myself to him if that is what you're asking." Even if they had come so very close to doing so multiple times. She closed her eyes, thankful for that small mercy at least. To spend the rest of her life knowing him more intimately than she already did was a pain she knew she would suffer through forever.

"May I be excused?" she asked.

"Of course," her father said.

Hailey could feel both their gazes on her as she walked from the room. She was strong, intelligent, and capable. She could get through this pain. Right now, it was raw and new, jagged, and left her cut and broken, but it would pass. In time she would be her old self again.

She just needed to give herself time.

CHAPTER
TWENTY-SEVEN

Greyson sat in the ducal carriage, his stomach in a knot of nerves. He was minutes from the Woodville estate, ready to throw himself at Hailey's feet, not only for forgiveness for what happened with his father, but his unwitting part in the duke's despicable revenge plan.

He took a calming breath, told himself she would forgive him. She wouldn't kick him back to London and ask him to stay there. "Her feelings will not be changed," he said aloud. "She will forgive me."

The carriage turned onto the Woodville drive and not soon after pulled up in front of the modest estate. Another carriage was parked before the pretty sandstone home, young Luke holding the horse's reins while whoever was inside visited.

Greyson jumped down, waving to Luke whose eyes bulged at the sight of him. He shyly waved back, and Greyson smiled, having always liked the young lad. He could understand his shock at knowing who he was now.

He doubted that few in the county knew he was now the Duke of Derby.

He strode up to the door, knocking and smiling in welcome at Molly, one of the maids in the house who answered. Her expression was similar to Luke's, her eyes wide and conversation mute. She stepped aside, letting him in, and he passed her his card. "The Duke of Derby to see Miss Hailey Woodville if she is at home."

Molly nodded, shutting the door before dipping into an awkward curtsy. "Of course, Your Grace. There are other visitors, so please wait here while I speak to Miss Woodville."

"Of course." He cooled his heels in the foyer of the house. Feeling eyes on himself, he glanced up and spotted several other Woodville sisters, the second oldest, Isla's, less than welcoming.

His heart lurched at the sight of them, all of who had similarities to Hailey. The reminder of her made him miss her all the more.

Molly came back into the foyer. "This way, if you please, Your Grace. They are having tea in the parlor."

Greyson followed the maid and steeled himself at the sight of Mr. Martin Bagshaw and a woman he had not seen before, his eyes skimming over everyone else in attendance until they landed on Hailey.

She sat on a chair, the sunlight streaming through the windows behind her, giving her an ethereal effect. She was so beautiful, and an overwhelming need to kiss her, to hold her tight raged through him.

"Your Grace," Mrs. Woodville said, standing and giving him the barest of curtsies. "We are just taking tea with Mr. Bagshaw, whom I'm certain you remember. We must congratulate him as he's now engaged."

His gut clenched, and he frowned. What the blazes! They were engaged? "You're engaged to Miss Woodville?" He could not hide the shock from his tone. "Well, I should probably have written first before coming here."

The lips of the young woman beside Mr. Bagshaw thinned in displeasure. "Why would the Duke of Derby think such a thing, Martin?" she asked Bagshaw, who had turned bright red.

Hailey stood, clasping her hands at her front. "You are mistaken, Your Grace. Mr. Bagshaw is betrothed to Miss Susan Withers. They formed an attachment after the Grafton ball and are paying calls today since the wedding is one week from now."

Relief poured through Greyson, and he strode up to Bagshaw who reluctantly stood and shook his hand. "Congratulations to you both." He turned his attention to Hailey. It was hard not to see that his being here was not welcome. There was a hardness behind her eyes, and he hated that he had placed it there. He wanted her to look at him as she always had—with amusement, pleasure, and above all, happiness.

I will not leave here without her love.

"I wonder why you are here, Your Grace?" Mr. Bagshaw asked. "Surely you do not think that you are worthy of Miss Woodville's hand after all your father's atrocious behavior toward this family. The numerous lies your father inflicted upon this family, causing them shame."

Greyson narrowed his eyes, uncertain what Bagshaw meant by his words, as he had only been privy to the disagreement they had at the Grafton Town Hall. So unless the staff was telling tales in town, the man was merely annoyed that he was here for Miss Woodville.

"I fail to see how my being here and wishing to speak to

Miss Woodville has anything to do with you," he drawled. "Have I not just been told you're betrothed to the lovely Miss Withers?" He smiled at the young woman, and she blushed. Already Greyson knew the lady was too good for Bagshaw.

"Of course, but Miss Woodville is my friend," Bagshaw sputtered.

Greyson raised one suspicious brow. "If you did not want Miss Woodville to become attached to another, you should not have offered to marry anyone else. Mayhap you are not so loyal to her since you did not offer to marry her again after the altercation at the town ball. Were you worried the Woodville reputation was tarnished forever and therefore yours by association?"

He turned back to Hailey, taking her hand. "Walk with me. We should speak." Her eyes darted to her parents before she relented. "We will talk in the library."

Greyson followed her from the room, glaring at Bagshaw on his way out. The pompous fool. If he regretted his choice, it was not his fault. If he were angry at anyone, he ought to be angry at himself for choosing the wrong woman to marry, for there was no one as perfect and as sweet as Hailey.

She held the library door open and then closed it the moment he stepped inside, walking over to her father's desk and leaning against the wood. She crossed her arms over her chest, her face shuttered and hard.

Greyson took a calming breath and prepared himself for battle. He would win her. There was no other choice.

"You look beautiful today, Hailey," he said, reaching for her. She pushed his hands away, going about the desk and sitting on her father's chair. "What are you doing here, Your Grace?"

He loathed that she would not call him by his name. He was still getting used to his title, but he never wished to be known as duke or Your Grace with Hailey. Only Greyson.

"I have come back to win your heart. I..."

She laughed, the sound thick with sarcasm. "Really, have you now. What a pity you could not find your voice when your father was in this very room telling us all how much we resembled pond scum and that I was practically a whore who plied her trade in Grafton instead of the docks in London."

He sat on the chair opposite her, leaning across the desk. "I did not know what he had planned. I had no knowledge that he ever courted your mama or that she denied him her hand, and he sought revenge on her. That he had stripped her family of their fortune. I knew none of that."

"So why were you in Grafton if not as one of your father's minions?" she asked, watching him keenly.

"As I said, I was sent here as punishment for what he termed lewd behavior. My father hated anyone who enjoyed anything. His sole purpose in life was to make others despair of being around him. As his son, I could not escape, not at least until he sent me here."

"Explain to me, so I understand."

He swallowed, needing her to comprehend. "I did have a mistress, for I did not want the complications of courting anyone in London and making her my wife. No one had sparked an interest in me. A mistress made my life easier; there were no emotions, just transactions between two people. She did not ask anything of me, and I did not feel like I had to give her any more than her fee." He cringed, hating what was coming out of his mouth. "I know that sounds cold and unfeeling, but it was better than marrying a woman I did not love."

"Had you really parted from your mistress when we first kissed?" she asked, concern in her tone.

"My father dismissed her, but I did ensure before I left London that she was taken care of before she could find another protector."

"That is something, I suppose," she said. "Is that all you wished to talk to me about or was there more before you leave?"

"Hailey," he said, his tone beseeching. "It was not until I met you that my heart lurched in my chest. That for the first time, I had found someone who did not know who I was or what I would bring to a marriage. You saw me as common Mr. Greyson Everett. A man with little to his name, and yet the man who held your heart for a time. I was the richest of men. Please marry me, Hailey. I need you to be my wife, my lover, and my duchess. You are the only person who loved me for me, not for who I was, and I cannot live without that. I will not live without it."

She pursed her lips, narrowing her eyes in thought before she leaned over the table, tapping her fingers atop the mahogany. "You will not live without it? Is that a threat or a demand, Your Grace?"

"A plea." He stood and came around the desk, kneeling before her. He took her hands and held them, squeezing them in the hopes she would believe what he said. "I love you, Hailey Woodville. I love all of you. The autocratic gentleman's daughter who is not afraid to order me about, to chastise me when I'm out of place, or meet me under a willow tree when in need of my kisses." She blushed, and he lifted her hand, kissing her long, slender fingers.

"I adore that you wanted to fight for a man who was not

your equal, and even here and now, before you as a duke, I'm not worthy. I know that. I should have booted my father out the day he came here. I should have defended you better. I have no excuse other than I was as shocked as you were at what he said. Please know that before he died, I had told him that I would marry you. That I did not care for his title or his wealth, that I would go to you, marry you with nothing if you would have me."

"But he died before you could come here and say all that," she stated, watching him. "How do I know that is true?"

He nodded. "He did die before I could come here, and therefore you have to choose to believe me or not. I was informed of his death the next morning."

"And Lady Francesca? We read that you were promenading about in Hyde Park with her. Are you certain you do not want to marry her instead?"

Damn it all to hell. He had no idea such gossip had reached this far north. "Although the betrothal was not announced in *The Times* due to my father's lawyer merely forgetting to place the advertisement, Lady Francesca had been informed by our fathers that the marriage would go ahead. I felt obliged to call on her, explain what had happened, and I begged her to break the contract."

"And did she?" Hailey asked him, and for the first time since his arrival, he spotted a flicker of fear in her green eyes.

"No, she did not. But a handsome sum of money soon changed her father's mind when I found he owed several thousand to various gentlemen about town. Lady Francesca's dowry is restored, and her father will not go to debtors' prison, and I do not have to marry her."

Hailey sighed, her fingers tightening against his. "Well

then," she paused, "I suppose since you're apologizing, I should too."

"What do you have to apologize for?" he asked.

A small smile lifted her lips, and hope burst through his chest. She let go of his hands, sliding them about his neck instead. "Because if I'm to be your wife and duchess, that will be punishment enough for you for the rest of your life."

Greyson wrenched her off the chair and settled her on his lap, holding her close. "Marrying you will be no punishment. I love you so very dearly, and you showed me how to love. Before meeting you, I never thought that I could care for anyone, but your chastisement, then friendship, and eventually love showed me differently." Greyson reached into his pocket, pulling out his mother's ring, a large, square diamond that every Duchess of Derby had worn from the moment of her betrothal. He held it up to her, meeting her gaze. "Marry me, my beautiful, darling Hailey. Be my wife, the mother of my children. And, if God is willing, be the love of my life, in this one and all the rest."

She blinked, and tears slipped down her cheeks. Greyson kissed them away, beseeching her to say yes.

Hailey glanced at the ring and sniffed, holding out her finger. He slipped it on, pleased that it fit her perfectly. "I will marry you, Greyson. I love you so much," she said.

He took her lips in a kiss that entwined their families from this day forward. She laughed, and he did too as they sealed their promise. Contentment and utter happiness settled over him for the first time in his life. No one could rip them apart, and no one could tell them what they could or couldn't do.

She would be his duchess, and he her duke from this day on and always forever after.

TWENTY-EIGHT

"Come with me."

Hailey started at the sound of Greyson's voice that floated through a partially opened window at her back. She glanced over her shoulder and spied him, hiding out of sight, and fought not to laugh.

They were not supposed to see each other tonight. In fact, Greyson was believed to be at a nearby manor house he had rented for the month leading up to their wedding.

Hailey excused herself from the small gathering in the drawing room and proceeded toward the terrace doors. With everyone enjoying the lively conversation and excitement over their wedding tomorrow, she slipped out without notice and ran quickly to where she had seen him.

He met her halfway, kissing her quickly before pulling her toward the lawns.

"I have two horses, and I'm stealing you away."

She pulled on his hand, halting him. "But it's considered bad luck to see me before the wedding. And if Mama finds out that you've taken me anywhere, she'll take the opportunity to scold me one last time before I become your wife."

He laughed, his arms enfolding her and hoisting her against his chest. Hailey sighed, taking the opportunity to feel him. Although she had seen him yesterday, it was already too many hours gone.

"I have a champagne picnic set up for you at the manor house. Please, tell me you will come. I have missed you."

His cajoling tone broke down her denial, and she nodded. "Very well, but only a few drinks. I want to feel my best for tomorrow."

His wicked grin made her stomach twist in expectation. "Oh, you will, my love. I will ensure you have nothing but a pleasurable day."

They rode over to the estate. Thankfully the moonlight did not make the journey too hazardous. The windows of the house Greyson had leased were beacons of light as they came toward it. A footman stood outside, and two stable lads were ready to take their horses.

No sooner had she slid off her mount had Greyson dragged her into the house and up the stairs. "Greyson, I cannot go to your room. What will people think?"

He shrugged, hoisting her up into his arms and carrying her along the hall. "Greyson, what are you doing?" She laughed as he stepped into a large, masculine room. The bed was massive. The rich-green bedding matched the window dressings that hung from ceiling to floor.

He set her down and closed the door, the snick of the lock loud in the room. Hailey crossed her arms, raising one suspicious brow. "Are you trying to seduce me before our wedding, Your Grace?"

He scoffed, going to where two glasses of champagne were poured and handing her one. She sipped, the fruity, refreshing drink just what she needed. "Of course not. I've already seduced you, so I cannot do so again."

Hailey grinned, begging to differ, and instead strolled about the room, passing the platter of fruit and picking up a strawberry. "Just think, from tomorrow, we shall share a room just like this one for the rest of our lives. Are you ready to be a husband, Your Grace?"

He set down his glass of champagne and moved toward her. He reminded her of a predator about to pounce on its prey. But unlike most, Hailey wanted to be sprung upon and caught. Especially by the man she loved.

"Greyson, not Your Grace. I'm Greyson to you, your husband from tomorrow, never Your Grace. We are only that to others."

Hailey set her glass down also and wrapped her arms around his neck. "So now that you have me here, what are we going to do, Greyson?" She let her finger trace down his neck, chest and then settle on the hem of his breeches. His eyes darkened with need. A need that she, too, felt.

He kissed her, took her mouth in a kiss so unlike any others they had shared since their betrothal. His tongue tangled with hers, his hands ripped at her gown, stripping her bare before the bed. She could feel the tension in his body, the need to claim her as his own.

Hailey's hands could not keep from him. She dragged his shirt off over his head, kissing his neck and chest, her tongue circling his nipple.

His fingers spiked into her hair, tightening her curls into his fist to keep her near him. He groaned when her hand slid over the front of his breeches, his cock hard and long against her palm.

"I want you, Greyson. Tonight. I cannot wait another day."

He ripped his falls open, shuffling off his breeches. He picked her up, and she wrapped her legs about his waist, undulating against him, soothing the ache between her legs that he always evoked.

He groaned through the kiss, and they fell onto the bed in a tangle of arms and legs. She could feel him at her core, teasing her with his cock. She pushed up against him, seeking release as only he knew how to give her.

"You are impatient, my love. But do not worry, you'll get what you want."

She shook her head, clasping his jaw in her hands. "You sought me out, remember? If anyone is impatient, it is you."

He threw her a wicked grin, pushing a little ways inside. She thought she would feel pain. Odd—even at his intrusion, she did not. If anything, she felt nothing but need and realized that there were more wonderful things to come when they joined fully.

"We shall agree to both be as impatient as each other." He pushed farther into her. He was long and thick. Her core ached, and if she were as innocent as she once was, she would have been embarrassed by how wet he made her. But not anymore. Now she knew what that meant, that he made her want him, a sign of just how much.

She shoved his chest, rolled him onto his back, and impaled herself on his manhood. Her moan mingled with his gasp, and she sat there a moment, relishing the feel of him inside.

His fingers clasped her hips. "Ride me, take your pleasure, my love." He swore when she did as he ordered.

Hailey rolled her hips, lifting herself up and down on his manhood, which he seemed to enjoy. He thrust into her, giving as much as taking. She could feel herself moving, sliding toward release, but this time it would be different.

This time it was not his mouth or hand that brought her pleasure. This time they were giving each other mutual satisfaction. She ran her hands over his chest, reveled in the beat of his heart beneath her palm.

"Damn it, Hailey. Come for me." His voice was deep and gravelly.

She rode him harder, moved against him, and took what she wanted. He shifted the angle of his thrusts, and he hit a part of her deep inside that made her moan. She threw her head back, lost herself in the feel of him, joined as they were.

He rolled them, coming over her, pinning her hands above her head. He thrust hard, over and over, his eyes wild with need, dark and focused on giving her what she wanted.

Him.

Hailey wrapped her legs around him, letting him take her, and pleasure burst through her like light. It pulsed, thrummed with exquisite bliss. Greyson moaned her name. He spent, his seed settling deep inside her womb.

He flopped beside her, pulling her into the crook of his arm, their breathing ragged, and Hailey took a moment to calm her racing heart. She had never been with Greyson like that before, but she knew that from tonight onward, she would never get tired of what they had just shared.

She idly played with the hairs on his chest, reveling in the feel of his taut muscles that she loved so very much. "However am I going to go home now? I want to stay here in your arms until tomorrow."

He chuckled, kissing her temple. "I shall have the carriage hitched to take you home before your parents send out a search party for you. Although I'm sure they would only need to hazard a guess of where you went."

True, her parents had been quite understanding of her affections for Greyson and his toward her and had let them sit alone in the parlor or take walks unchaperoned this past month. The happiest of her life.

"Do not be late for the church tomorrow," he said, turning to face her.

She grinned up at him. "I will not be. I promise."

"Very good." He kissed her again, and fire coursed through her blood. He rolled over her, and Hailey lost herself in his arms yet again. It was not until dawn kissed the hills of Northamptonshire that the ducal carriage rolled to a halt before the Woodville Estate and wedding preparations for the Duke of Derby and Miss Hailey Woodville could start in earnest.

EPILOGUE

Greyson watched as his duchess spoke to several of their friends, pleased to see that no matter what his concerns may have been regarding her being the daughter of a gentleman, none of that seemed to bother anyone, which he was pleased about. He did not want to make enemies in his life, but he would have should anyone slight or say anything rude to his wife.

He sipped his wine, watching her, knowing the secret they carried that no one else was privy to. Soon they would be a family of three, and he could not wait to meet his son or daughter.

His good friend Cyrus, Marquess of Chilsten, came up to him, handing him a glass of whisky. "Thought you may like something stronger," he said. He stood beside him, watching the throng of dancers.

"Thank you." He finished his wine before handing his empty glass to a passing footman. "I have not seen you since the wedding. I heard you took part in a house party after our nuptials but have not been seen or heard from since."

"I have been occupied elsewhere." His friend nodded toward Mr. and Mrs. Woodville, who stood with one of Hailey's younger sisters, Julia.

"Who is that young woman? She looks familiar," Chilsten said, a contemplating light in his eyes.

"My sister-in-law, Miss Julia Woodville. She's not officially out yet, but Hailey did not think to keep her home while everyone went out this evening. They're in town finishing the season with us."

Chilsten nodded. "Ah yes, very good." He paused. "They are all a very handsome family. I can see why you picked your duchess, Your Grace."

Greyson smiled, catching Hailey's eye across the room. A mischievous light entered hers, and he wondered what his wicked minx was thinking. However, he could fathom a guess. "I'm very fortunate that my father punished me in the way he did, and I ended up at the Woodville Estate. I shudder to think of what my life could have been had I not met Her Grace."

Chilsten clapped him on the back. "Congratulations again. Now, if you'll excuse me, there is another Woodville whom I must meet."

Greyson watched him stride over toward Julia Woodville and did not miss the annoyance that flittered across her visage. If Chilsten thought the chit would be an easy conquest, he would be vastly disappointed.

He laughed just as Hailey came up to him, linking her arm with his. "What are you chuckling at, husband?" she asked.

"It seems your sister Julia has an admirer."

Hailey looked across the ballroom floor to see Julia dipping into a curtsy and looking anywhere but at Lord Chilsten. "Julia looks less than pleased by the introduction."

Greyson chuckled, pulling his wife closer. "I think out of all your sisters, Julia is my favorite."

Hailey raised her brow, looking up at him. "Really, and why is that?" she asked.

"Because she looks the most like you and has a fiery light within her that will make her hard to catch. Anyone who looks to make her his bride will have to work hard, and Chilsten likes nothing more than a good challenge."

She grinned. "I wish him well then."

Greyson watched her, unable to tear his eyes from the splendid vision she made. In the six months since their marriage, she had not changed, not inwardly in any case. Of course, her dresses were of the finest silk and chiffon and muslin. And she wore a tiara to most London balls and had access to the ducal family jewels. But when they were alone, at home, no matter if that was here in London or their estate in Kent, she soon reverted to the country lass he fell in love with and whom she seemed most comfortable being.

She had blended into his world without a hiccup, and he into hers. She was simply perfect.

"Why are you looking at me like that, Greyson?" she asked him, tipping her head to the side.

He took the opportunity, leaned down, and kissed her. She did not pull away, embarrassed by his public display of affection. Instead, she kissed him back, her fingers tangling into the lapels of his coat and keeping him right where he wanted to be.

Gasps sounded about the room, and it wasn't until she laughed that he pulled away.

"I love you so much," he whispered for only her to hear.

She grinned, running her hand across his jaw. "And I, you," she said, kissing him quickly. "Forever."

He nodded. "Absolutely."

Dear Reader,

Thank you for taking the time to read *A Duke of a Time*! I hope you enjoyed the first book in my Wayward Woodvilles series!

I'm forever grateful to my readers, and if you're able, I would appreciate an honest review of *A Duke of a Time*. As they say, feed an author, leave a review!

Alternatively, you can keep in contact with me by visiting my website, subscribing to my newsletter or following me online. You can contact me at www.tamarag-ill.com.

Happy reading!

Tamara Gill

Wayward Woodvilles

Series starts Feb, 2022
Pre-order your copy today!

SERIES BY TAMARA GILL

The Wayward Woodvilles

Royal House of Atharia

League of Unweddable Gentlemen

Kiss the Wallflower

Lords of London

To Marry a Rogue

A Time Traveler's Highland Love

A Stolen Season

Scandalous London

High Seas & High Stakes

Daughters Of The Gods

Stand Alone Books

Defiant Surrender

To Sin with Scandal

Outlaws

About the Author

Tamara is an Australian author who grew up in an old mining town in country South Australia, where her love of history was founded. So much so, she made her darling husband travel to the UK for their honeymoon, where she dragged him from one historical monument and castle to another.

A mother of three, her two little gentlemen in the making, a future lady (she hopes) and a part-time job keep her busy in the real world, but whenever she gets a moment's peace she loves to write romance novels in an array of genres, including regency, medieval and time travel.

www.tamaragill.com